A RARE TWEET

"Your commanding officer, young man," Lucy demanded.

"Well, lady, I—"

Lucy interrupted him vigorously. "Please don't call me 'lady.' My mother once had a deranged collie named Lady. She tormented chickens and children. Call me Lucy. Or call me Miss Wayles."

The desk sergeant didn't call her anything. He said, "I am afraid he's not available right now. Perhaps I can help you."

"Then," Lucy said, "I would appreciate if you'd point me toward the officers who are investigating the murder of Abraham Lescalles."

"You mean the bird-watcher."

"Exactly."

"That would be Detective Loach. I'll try to get him down to see you."

Ten minutes later a tall, stooped man with a beautifully bald head approached. He said simply, "I'm Loach."

"I'm Wayles," Lucy said, playing the game. "I have important information about the Lescalles murder. It was," Lucy announced, "definitely not what it seemed."

THE DR. NIGHTINGALE MYSTERY SERIES
BY LYDIA ADAMSON

Beware the Tufted Duck

A Lucy Wayles Mystery

by

Lydia Adamson

A SIGNET BOOK

SIGNET
Published by the Penguin Group
Penguin Books USA Inc., 375 Hudson Street,
New York, New York 10014, U.S.A.
Penguin Books Ltd, 27 Wrights Lane,
London W8 5TZ, England
Penguin Books Australia Ltd, Ringwood,
Victoria, Australia
Penguin Books Canada Ltd, 10 Alcorn Avenue,
Toronto, Ontario, Canada M4V 3B2
Penguin Books (N.Z.) Ltd, 182–190 Wairau Road,
Auckland 10, New Zealand

Penguin Books Ltd, Registered Offices:
Harmondsworth, Middlesex, England

First published by Signet, an imprint of Dutton Signet,
a division of Penguin Books USA Inc.

First Printing, October, 1996
10 9 8 7 6 5 4 3 2 1

 REGISTERED TRADEMARK—MARCA REGISTRADA

Printed in the United States of America

PUBLISHER'S NOTE
This is a work of fiction. Names, characters, places, and incidents either are the
product of the author's imagination or are used fictitiously, and any resemblance to
actual persons, living or dead, events, or locales is entirely coincidental.

Chapter 1

I know Miss Lucy Wayles to be a kind, gentle, intelligent, gracious, loving, self-sacrificing, and, above all, sensible Southern lady.

After all, one of her distant ancestors was a distant cousin of Thomas Jefferson's wife's father.

Lucy Wayles pushed too far or too fast, however, is another story entirely.

Pushed too far or too fast, she will quickly turn into one of Quantrill's Raiders loosed upon the Big Apple.

I saw just such a transformation occur on a pretty March day in New York City. It happened on the steps of the Queens County Courthouse.

The judge had dismissed all eleven misdemeanor charges against Lucy for her activities on the Fifty-ninth Street Bridge back in January. She took the verdict very much in her stride. In fact, it was clear that I had worried more about her fate than she had.

Happily, the proceedings were behind us now. And arm in arm we walked down the white stone courthouse steps. There was a distant hint of spring in the air. A lovely day—a little brisk, a little mild—had become even lovelier, because Lucy had her freedom.

Lucy cut a splendid figure walking down those steps: antique military jacket; long dress; short-cut white hair; her small purse held tightly in front of her as she walked.

Of course she was wearing those fearsome-looking construction boots with the thick crepe soles. I hated them, and found they ruined her smart outfits. But, as Lucy always said when I cast a disapproving glance down at her feet, "Markus, you never know."

Oh, but I did know. I knew she meant that she might at any time have to plunge into some odd terrain to evaluate a bird sighting—maybe even swampy Jamaica Bay on the rumor of an elusive black rail nest.

Suddenly, from behind us, we heard a grating voice: "Miss Wayles! Miss Lucy Wayles!"

We stopped and looked back. The deep throat belonged to a harrowingly thin young man who held a spiral notebook. On his jacket lapel was an oversized press identification badge.

Lucy turned to face the street again. I followed suit.

"Oh, my dear Lord," she said unhappily. "It's a reporter, Markus."

"But only one, Lucy," I replied, trying to hearten her. "Remember how many there were on the bridge? And television cameras?"

The reporter circled in front of us and blocked our way.

"I'm Chuck Cavaretta from *Your Town.* I just want to ask a few questions."

Lucy said nothing.

"Were you surprised at the judge's decision?" he asked.

It was one of the least intelligent questions I had heard from a member of the press in some time.

"Surprised?" Lucy hooted. "What an asinine question!"

"I mean . . . surely you were expecting some fines . . . at least . . . or something . . . at least."

"I was innocent of all charges," Lucy said.

I caught in her voice the Southern twang that always came out when her slow burn was starting. The madder she got, the deeper the twang and the deeper the voice.

"But you tied up one of the city's major thoroughfares for almost five hours. You created havoc on the bridge. And all because of a ridiculous duck."

Lucy was silent.

The reporter pressed his point. "The whole city was asking: Who is this crazy grandmother? You almost killed yourself climbing that iced girder. Even your bird-watching club kicked you out as president after that. How can you say you were innocent of all charges?"

Lucy's voice had dropped into basso profundo range by the time she started to speak.

"Young man," she said solemnly, "first of all, I am grandmother to no one.

"Second, I am not, as you so sensitively labeled it, crazy. I am the former director of the Archives of Urban Natural History of the City of New York. I was hired right out of the university library in Chapel Hill, North Carolina, in 1968 to come to New York and catalogue a small collection. It is now one of the great specialized libraries in the world, attached to the Museum of Natural History. I have commendations from five mayors. And I was voted Librarian of the Year by the Special Libraries Association—on three occasions, I might add.

"Third. It is true that I was asked to resign my presidency of the Central Park Bird-watchers. And it is true that they claimed I was relieved of my duties because of irresponsible behavior. But what they claim to be true and what is true are two different things. In fact, there were long-standing differences within that organization, if one can call it an organization. And I am now the elected president of the Olmsted's Irregulars and many former members of the Central Park Bird-watchers have joined me."

I squirmed a bit. Election? What election?

"Four. It was not, as you say, a ridiculous duck on that bridge. It was a *tufted duck*. A striking white-and-black male. A very rare visitor to this side of the Atlantic. And he had been overcome by the frigid weather."

She stopped suddenly, smiled sweetly at the flabbergasted reporter, opened her purse, removed her compact, opened it, looked, shut it, placed it back into her purse, and continued.

"Five. You are an alleged pressman, I believe. Well, your priorities are skewed—alarmingly so. There must be any number of bills in the city council today, passage or failure of which would affect the lives of millions. Yet you stand here asking vapid questions of what you clearly regard as a dotty old grandmother and planning to write an insulting article about the concerns of a dedicated bird-watcher who harms no one—all for a journal that in truth is little more than a supermarket giveaway.

"Six. You must ask one of the more fashionable young people at your place of employment where to obtain a decent haircut.

"And, finally, young man, let me give you a piece of advice. Beware the tufted duck!"

Then she turned to me, took my arm, and suggested: "Shall we go, Markus?"

Poor Mr. Cavaretta was left standing there in the dust, so to speak.

We strolled south on Queens Boulevard.

"There is much to do, Markus," she said.

"Is there?"

She opened her eyes wide, as if astonished at my response.

"Didn't I tell you that Peter Marin called me? There's been a sighting of an eastern phoebe near that funny-looking willow in the Upper Lobe. We'll go there this afternoon. If confirmed, it means spring is truly here, Markus. Isn't that wonderful!"

"Yes, Lucy, wonderful."

I tried to process all the information she had given me. The only reason I became a bird-watcher was because I believed it would help me in my courtship of Lucy Wayles—a courtship that has been, so far, singularly unsuccessful. Oh, of course I've come to admire the birds and the birders, but I'm slow on the uptake. I knew that the eastern phoebe was in the tyrant flycatcher family . . . that it lived on flying insects . . . and that the Upper Lobe was a pond in Central Park. But that's about all. I wouldn't know a phoebe if it landed on my head.

"But first things first, Markus. I have the most powerful hankering for a Linzer torte and I seem to recall there's a wonderful Austrian cafe a mere ten blocks from here."

It was something of a hike, ten blocks on those rambling Queens sidewalks. But an authentic Austrian café? I'd gladly walk twenty. Lucy and I shared a great many enthusiasms. Desserts were near the top of the list.

We found the café and Lucy ordered her treat. As we were sitting there, I asked, "What did you mean when you told that reporter 'Beware the tufted duck!'?"

"I don't know what I meant, Markus. It just popped into my head. That's all. Hasn't that ever happened to you, Markus?"

"Not often," I confessed.

"Actually, it would have made more sense if I had told him, 'Beware the Rieffer's hummingbird.'"

"Why?"

"As you well know, Markus, almost fifty percent of their nesting failures is the result of the stealing of nest materials by other hummingbirds."

The blank look on my face must have been pathetic. She tried to ease my perplexity.

"By which I mean that the truth is often stolen by . . . how shall I put it? . . . by the unrighteous."

"Ah," I said, feigning enlightenment.

She concentrated on the torte. I observed her happily. She was one of those rare eaters who somehow combined fastidiousness and gusto. She had launched a full frontal attack on the torte—but primly.

Just watching her made me hungry.

I ordered a napoleon. She raised her eyebrows in consternation but said nothing until the pastry was placed in front of me.

Then: "Markus, I have never understood your fascination with those things."

"What things?" I asked, my fork poised.

She pointed in mild distaste at my pastry.

How can one explain something like that? Either you love that tooth-numbing icing and those dark chocolate swirls or you don't. "I can't explain it, Lucy. Perhaps it's the custard that attracts me. Or the flaky, butter-drenched layers of dough. I don't know! I've always loved napoleons."

"From childhood?"

I thought for a while, staring at the pastry.

"No, not from childhood. I never saw one when I was a child."

"Well, go on, Markus. Eat it!"

I began to eat.

"Did you ever meet my aunt Hattie, Markus? The one from Tennessee?" she asked.

"How could I? Your relatives never come to New York."

"Well, she once said that the three most dangerous things on earth are a preacher who drinks, a dog who won't eat table scraps, and French pastry."

"Your aunt Hattie might well be a sage," I noted.

The napoleon was celestial. I tried not to show too much delight.

"Yes, Hattie is smart—sage, even, as you say. But she can be dangerous."

"How so?" I asked, putting down my fork and deflaking the surroundings with my napkin.

"It's hard to describe. She reminds me of a peregrine falcon."

I picked up the fork and continued ravishing my napoleon, then put the utensil down.

"Do you remember those peregrines we saw over the Palisades?" she asked.

"Yes. Last year."

"No, no. It was two years ago. We saw two of them flying together . . . high above the cliffs . . . going north. Remember how smoothly they went . . . short, powerful wing strokes. And every once in a while they would glide on a thermal—higher, always higher. Do you remember what happened next, Markus?"

"To be honest, Lucy, I don't."

"Oh, you must remember how one of them suddenly stooped! How one of them dived so suddenly and with such speed that it took your breath away! How it slammed into its prey—a mourning dove who was flying south along the rim of the cliffs so innocently! Do you remember it now, Markus?"

"Yes," I replied.

Lucy's eyes misted over. She seemed far away—on the cliffs again.

"But what does this have to do with your dangerously wise aunt Hattie?"

Lucy came back to the present. "She is a very kind

lady, but every once in a while she attacks verbally, without warning, suddenly, like a peregrine's stoop."

"I trust she doesn't eat mourning doves."

"Not as a *steady* diet, Markus."

After the Austrian treats we took a cab back to Manhattan. I dropped Lucy first, in front of the old brownstone on Ninety-third Street, just east of Fifth Avenue. She lived alone in a small apartment on the second floor with four large windows overlooking the street. Then the cab dropped me on Fifty-seventh and Ninth. I live alone in a luxuriously outsized six-room apartment—six large rooms—in a landmark building.

At three-thirty that afternoon, I met Lucy, as planned, in front of the Church of the Heavenly Dove, on Ninetieth and Fifth Avenue.

Our fellow avian enthusiast Peter Marin was also there. He is a large, middle-aged redhead who always wears Li'l Abner denim overalls into the park. Rumor had it that he was a very successful freelance commercial artist who never left his triplex apartment on Seventy-ninth Street except for bird-watching excursions.

He, along with Beatrice Plumb and John Wu, had defected to Olmsted's Irregulars from the Central Park Bird-watchers group because of their loyalty and respect for Lucy.

We entered the park, skirted the reservoir, and walked west past Belvedere Lake and the Delacorte Theatre.

Peter was carrying his expensive and very powerful, super-duper high-tech Carl Zeiss 8X56 binoculars. I had borrowed them once, so I knew they weighed a ton.

Lucy had her small green waterproof pair of Leica's.

I had my ugly Navy surplus binoculars in a cracked leather case slung over one shoulder.

"Did you see the eastern phoebe yourself, Peter?" Lucy asked.

"No! Abraham called me this morning. He told me he was out in the park very early."

Abraham Lescalles was a wildly passionate bird-watcher who had great respect for Lucy but had refused to "jump ship" and join Olmsted's Irregulars. "Too old and too set in my ways," he had explained apologetically.

"I miss Abraham," Lucy said.

As we approached the Upper Lobe, which was simply an extension of the Boating Lake, Lucy shifted into her birding mode. It was wonderful to watch. She began to walk leaning forward like a hunter looking for tracks on the ground and in the sky, scanning the entire horizon continually. She kept her hands at her sides, as if she were about to dance. For some reason, once she entered that birder mode, she seemed taller and thinner than she really was. When birding, she always wore a thoroughly ragged old barn jacket, black with a scarlet lining, corduroy slacks, and a headband that could have been a genuine relic from the Haight-Ashbury flower child era.

In the park, Lucy always carried a knapsack; in one of its pockets there was always a pack of stiff new index cards—held together by a ferocious rubber band. Ever the librarian, Lucy would carefully record each sighting on a single card in Magic Marker and then, later, transfer it to her life list. She was always threatening to purchase a laptop computer to replace the index cards.

We reached the slope that led to the Upper Lobe and clambered down. We were just north of the small bridge that spanned the neck between the main Boating Lake and the Lobe. The bridge led into the heavily wooded Ramble. The water in the Lobe was brackish from the melting snow and ice that had run off the slope.

"This is where we saw the blue heron last' fall," Peter whispered.

"And that must be the willow," Lucy said, also in an urgent whisper, pointing at a tree on the far side of the water. It was cracked and twisted, showing its struggle with the harsh winter.

We all raised our binoculars together and began the search for the eastern phoebe—who was, if not *the* harbinger of spring, at least one of them.

"Concentrate on the exposed branches," Lucy instructed. "They 'hawk' insects from off the branch."

Our concentration was immediately aborted by what seemed to be a drunken yell.

We lowered our glasses.

"It's a homeless man," Lucy said. "He's drunk."

What appeared to be a homeless man was, indeed, lying under the bridge on a piece of cardboard. He had no shoes or socks on and was wearing a filthy red vest. He kept waving his arms and mumbling, moaning unbearably, seemingly directing his cries at us.

"Peter, would you please tell that man to be quiet for a few minutes! Explain to him the importance of remaining quiet," Lucy requested.

Peter nodded and lumbered off until he was halfway between Lucy and the bridge. Then he did the silliest thing. He brought his finger to his lip in the universal sign of silence and said "Shhhh!" in the loudest way possible. As if the pathetic drunk were a noisy child in church.

Then Peter turned back to us. His face had suddenly become chalk-white.

"It's Abraham, Lucy! It's Abraham!"

Lucy and I ran, not stopping until we reached the bridge.

We stared down at the gurgling man. He *was* Abraham Lescalles. And the red vest was simply the front of his shirt stained with blood from his slashed chest and throat.

I looked at Lucy, frozen, pinned in place. I couldn't get my limbs or my brain to do a damn thing.

Lucy tore open a pocket of her knapsack. She removed a quarter and gave it to me. "There's a pay phone on the side of the Delacorte Theatre. Go there quickly. Call 911."

I took the coin and ran up the slope as best I could. I learned later that about the same time I slipped the quarter into the slot, Abraham Lescalles died, his head held in Lucy's lap.

We never did see an eastern phoebe that day.

Chapter 2

I was so engrossed in trying to count the number of people entering the church that I didn't even realize Lucy was talking to me.

Until I felt a sharp poke in my ribs.

"What? What?"

"You didn't hear a word I said," she scolded.

"I'm sorry. I was looking around."

"That may well be your biggest trouble in life, Markus. You look but you don't see. Anyway, I was saying that when my time is up, I don't want a memorial service like this, or a procession to a cemetery. Just cremate me, crunch the remains into a suet block, and hang it between two trees for the crows."

She poked me again. "Can I depend on you?"

"Of course, Lucy."

She sat back in the very uncomfortable pew and smoothed her dress. It was a pretty garment, yet an impeccably appropriate mourning dress. I had never seen it before—it was made of thick black crepe with deep ridges. It had a high neck and muttonchop sleeves. The hem was at her ankles. Lucy looked rather like the announcer in a knife-throwing act.

Her hat was a black beret with two fake eagle feathers.

"Lucy," I asked, keeping my voice low, "why, do you suppose, have so many people showed up?"

She replied, "Abraham Lescalles was a much-loved man."

And she added, "And a pillar of the community."

I looked at her for a moment, incredulous. A pillar of the community? That was a bit much. Yes, Abraham Lescalles was a much-loved man. Yes, he had helped turn the Church of the Heavenly Dove into a community force—AA meetings, a feeding program for the homeless, guest speakers, cooking classes. But a *pillar of the community*? He was known as an occasional lecher. Even I knew that. And, in fact, he had once been banned from the church altogether for about a year because he had seduced a much younger parishioner. In addition, the lady in question was a married woman!

When I began to explain all this to Lucy, she only patted my hand.

The priest walked to the podium. The murmurs and buzzing died out.

He held out his hands dramatically and asked, "Do we know whom we have lost? Do we understand what has happened?"

He paused and looked out over the audience. "Like all tragedies," he continued, "this one has an inside and an outside. Like a grain of rice. With a husk and a kernel.

"The police have given us the husk. They say that our friend Abraham Lescalles was robbed of everything, including his shoes, and then slashed to death by a homemade knife. Two homeless men seen in the area are being sought for questioning. The knife was recovered from the scene.

"That, my friends, is the husk. But the kernel is—"

He had stopped suddenly. Some kind of commotion was taking place in the pew in front of us, toward the center aisle.

Then a woman stood up, gesturing wildly with her arms.

"Oh, my," Lucy said forlornly. "It's Sheila Ott."

The plump and quite pretty occasional bird-watcher looked like a madwoman.

Sheila called out, "Where is God's grace? Where is His grace? He has abandoned the city."

The crowd fell utterly silent. No one seemed to know what to do with the obviously distraught parishioner.

No one except Lucy. "Follow me, Markus," she said.

Lucy stood up, headed toward the aisle, and walked boldly into Sheila Ott's row. I followed, apologizing to the parishioners whose knees I was banging.

Sheila stared wildly at the intruder. Was she going to attack Lucy? I wondered.

But Lucy, fearless, just turned on a thousand-watt smile.

"Sheila, honey! What beautiful shoes you're wearing."

It was one of Lucy's more brilliant ploys. Sheila was totally confounded. She had stopped ranting and was staring down at her own feet.

Then Lucy took her by the hand and led her out of the church and onto Fifth Avenue.

Once outside, Sheila burst into sobs.

"It's not spring yet," Lucy said. "You probably got a chill this morning. I'm going to march you right over to my apartment and Markus here will make you some of his wonderful hot chocolate."

I rolled my eyes imploringly. Me? Make hot chocolate? I couldn't even deal with a tea bag. I started getting nervous. Was Lucy going to demand I treat the lady for shock? It was possible. No matter how many times I told her that I spent my medical career as a researcher into viral genetics—looking at the common cold and its ten thousand mutations through an electron microscope—she persisted in introducing me either as a retired internist or a heart specialist.

Actually, I do look like a kindly general practitioner.

Anyway, the three of us set off for Lucy's apartment, only three blocks away. Once inside, Lucy cleared a space on the sofa for Sheila, and then made room for me. This clearing was always necessary, since Lucy's ever-growing collections of books of all kinds, prints, maps, and index cards swamped the space.

The walls, however, were quite clear, except for the high bookcases and seven watercolors of birds, including one mesmerizing work of the garish roseate spoonbill.

I found myself looking around furtively for Dipper. That was Lucy's cat. A huge battleship-gray beast with white splotches. Lucy had found him two years ago on her way back from Hawk Mountain in Pennsylvania, where she'd gone to watch the raptor migration. He was on the roof of a Wa Wa convenience store. In fact, Lucy had first called him Wa Wa, but then she saw how he liked high places, so she changed his name to Big Dipper, and finally Dipper for short.

Lucy always told me that Dipper was the gentlest of pussycats. But he frightened the hell out of me. Particularly when I found him glaring down at me from one of his favorite perches on top of the shower curtain in the bathroom or on top of a kitchen cabinet or a bookcase.

Anyway, I didn't see him at all.

"Now, Sheila, don't you feel better?" Lucy asked, like a schoolmarm.

"He was such a wonderful man, Lucy! He would do anything for you. He loved the city. He loved the park. He loved the birds. Sure, he did some bad things. But we all do. We're only human."

I nodded knowingly in assent. Sheila was obviously talking about those old intimations of sexual promiscuity.

Lucy said, "All of us birders have a streak of libertinism."

That was news to me.

Then Sheila's round face went pale and tears welled up in her eyes. She brushed back the curls around her ears. She unbuttoned the top of her red jacket, as if it were a struggle to breathe. She was not only an attractive woman, today she looked terribly young . . . almost like a child . . . though I knew she was no spring chicken.

"What is the matter?" Lucy asked.

"You don't understand," Sheila gasped. "I am responsible for his murder."

Lucy stared at me. I stared back.

"What are you saying, dear?" asked Lucy.

"On the morning of the murder I heard reports that a long-eared owl had been sighted in a clump of evergreens behind the Metropolitan Museum of Art. I called Abraham and told him about it. He agreed to meet me behind the museum at four o'clock. So you see, in a sense I led him to his death. I pressed him to come there that day."

"Oh, no, no, no," Lucy countered. "He would have been in the park anyway."

"Why?"

"Well . . . tell me . . . did he show up at four o'clock?"

"No."

"I'll tell you why. Because Peter Marin had received a call from Abraham that morning. About an eastern phoebe in the Upper Lobe. He went there first that afternoon and was murdered before he could keep his appointment with you."

Then Lucy grasped Sheila's hands in her own. "He would have been in the park anyway. Don't you see, Sheila?"

She did. A weight seemed to drop away from her musculature. She cried again, this time tears of relief.

Five minutes later she was gone.

Lucy sat down on the sofa.

"Markus," she said, "why don't you be a good boy and make me some hot chocolate?"

"But I don't know how to make hot chocolate."

She didn't respond. We sat in silence. Finally I asked, "Is something bothering you?"

"Yes."

"What?"

"A feeling. A sense. A dread. A recipe of perplexity."

"You've lost me, Lucy."

"I once read a book by a clergyman from New England, Markus. He was a passionate birder. He said he was the most blessed of men because for more than twenty years he was able to breakfast to the song of the black-throated green warbler."

"So?"

"He never said what he ate for breakfast those twenty long years."

"I'm still lost, Lucy."

She leaned over and patted my hand but said nothing.

Suddenly there was a blur of gray and a light thud.

Dipper was now on top of one of the bookcases.

He draped himself over the wood like a fur stole and glared at me. Quite malevolently, I thought.

But Lucy said, "You see. I told you Dipper likes you."

Chapter 3

It was the third Thursday in April. One of those beautiful, bursting spring mornings.

The members of Olmsted's Irregulars gathered at the foot of the John Puroy Mitchell statue, inside the park at East Ninetieth Street.

I arrived at 6:55 A.M. Lucy and John Wu were already there.

Beatrice Plumb arrived at seven o'clock sharp and Peter Marin two minutes later.

Off we trudged along the horse path, heading south and west.

I always felt a rush of excitement when we started out. As if we were about to face great danger. It was a fantasy, of course, from my childhood, when I was addicted to books and movies about daring commando raids into Nazi-occupied Europe. Lucy was my brave French Resistance leader and I the American paratrooper.

Actually, our expedition that April morning was quite exciting, from a birder's point of view.

The warblers had arrived early on a strong and warm southern wind.

The Olmsted's Irregulars identified pine warblers, prairie warblers, Cape May warblers, Tennessee warblers, black-and-white warblers—to name just a few.

There was even an angry exchange between Peter Marin and the usually sedate Beatrice Plumb over whether one warbler in particular was a yellow-rump or yellow-throated variety. One being common and the other rare.

Even I had my moment of glory when I spotted and identified two brown-headed cowbirds on the limb of a cherry tree. They were obviously plotting some nest piracy, which is their modus operandi—letting other birds rear their young.

At nine o'clock in the morning we rested in what had become our traditional spot. This was a small, steep, wooded gully just west of the Balcony Bridge and just east of the West Seventy-seventh Street exit. The gully had originally been a conduit for a stream that led from the lake to the Ladies Pond. This pond had once been reserved for lady ice skaters, but then, alas, was paved over in the 1930s.

Our gully was not a place to wander around at night; its seclusion attracted various unsavory characters. But in the daytime it was fine.

We were all grungy and tired. The manic behavior of the warblers was infectious, but they were tiny creatures with lovely songs and we were huge creatures without much in the way of tunes.

So we sat down on whatever we could find—rocks and tree trunks, mostly—and peeled oranges and nibbled hard cheese and shared bananas.

I made sure my garbage bag was at the ready. That

was my responsibility: garbageman of Olmsted's Irregulars. I never knew whether to be proud of this assignment or not. But I did my job diligently; after all, Lucy always said, quoting some Zen master: "Leave no footprints on the earth. That is the first commandment."

Besides, there were many early gaffes I had to atone for—such as bringing a hot pastrami sandwich on my first birding expedition. This incident had already become legend. When Lucy introduces me to birders from afar, their eyes glaze over. They have heard! They know the story.

The snacks were consumed quickly, the garbage bag utilized, and then we were all on our feet again, ready to push on.

All except Lucy. She remained perched on a rock.

"What ails thee?" John Wu asked.

"Nothing ails me. I just want to say a few words."

John Wu bowed from the waist and recited sardonically, "You are the mother of us all."

So, we resettled in the gully and waited.

Lucy sighed heavily, smiled a mysterious smile, snapped her faded headband ever so delicately, and said: "I have been thinking about Abraham Lescalles."

Peter Marin released a tiny groan. But no one said a word.

What was there to say? Poor Abraham was dead and buried for many weeks now.

Lucy pressed on: "In particular, I am thinking about his shoes. The ones the police say were stolen by the murderers."

Everyone looked at everyone else. Shoes?

As for me, a little alarm bell went off in my head. Hadn't Lucy used a shoe ploy to get Sheila Ott out of that church? At the time it seemed to be a brilliant ploy. But maybe it wasn't that. Maybe Lucy had become a shoe fetishist.

"Do y'all remember his shoes?" she insisted.

Uh-oh. She was beginning to slip into down-home dialect.

But then, when no one answered, her voice became quite clipped and crisp.

"Let me help you remember them. You should. Abraham did have a 'thing' for them. Like a lot of birders do. I mean, John, I heard you wax poetic over your silly canvas boots. Anyway, Abraham always wore the worst-looking old pair of tattered white sneakers. I guess they were white once. They were in horrible shape. They were shredded, literally. As a matter of fact, he had to use two laces on each shoe. One to lace it up, the other to hold it together. Now . . . do you remember?"

"Yes. I remember. So what?" Beatrice Plumb replied.

"No one in his right mind would steal them," Lucy announced.

Peter Marin jumped in quickly. "The police say he was murdered by two homeless men. Homeless men are not necessarily in their right minds. And even if they were, people like that can't be too particular about the shoes they wear."

Lucy smiled at him in a patronizing fashion. "No one would steal those sneakers, Peter."

"What is it you are really saying, Lucy?" I finally asked, exasperated.

"Well, what I think is that the sneakers are still there."

"Where?"

"In the area where he was murdered."

"The police would have found them."

"They didn't look. They assumed the sneakers were taken with the money and the wallet."

"But they found the knife."

"So they did."

To make a long story short, five minutes later we had crossed West Drive and made our way down the slope. We stood in the clearing by the pond called the Upper Lobe.

It was exactly the spot where we had searched for the eastern phoebe and found poor Abraham Lescalles.

"Where do you propose we conduct this search?" Peter Marin asked.

"In the pond!" Lucy declared.

"I was afraid you were going to say that," he replied.

We stared glumly at the pond. It wasn't large . . . maybe twenty yards wide and forty yards long.

But except for the clearing in which we stood, the rest of the pond's banks were covered with thick brush and a thousand years of muck and mire.

"Markus and I will work our way east," Lucy declared.

"What about the snapping turtles?" Beatrice asked.

But it was too late for caution. We plunged into the search.

Each step was misery. And after each step we thrust our hands into the shallow murky water, along the edges of the pond. We retrieved often startling objects, but no sneakers.

Then tragedy struck. Beatrice Plumb fell into the pond. In his effort to help her, Peter Marin fell in after her.

When they emerged they were angry, and from across the pond Peter announced sullenly, "This search is over!"

We reassembled, bedraggled and defeated, in the clearing.

Lucy stood silently, hiding her disappointment well. When Lucy willed it, she could be the most gracious of women.

As for me, I decided to peel a tangerine for Beatrice to resurrect my image as a gallant.

Suddenly John Wu crouched like a gunfighter in a spaghetti Western.

"We are being watched," he whispered urgently.

By park rangers? Cops? Muggers? Homeless psychopaths?

No. A black-crowned night heron was blinking at us from a floating log in the pond.

"That might be Harry," John Wu said excitedly, forgetting everything else and bringing his binoculars up. "I remember him from last year."

John Wu, being a bond trader, naturally liked predatory birds.

As for me, I disliked night herons. They were the

ugliest of the heron family—squat with dull black, white, and gray markings.

But it wasn't their looks that made me queasy. Oh, no. After all, I am no great beauty. Nor was it their hunting ability, which was legendary. They hunted by sight—both wading and on the wing, dawn and dusk. And they ate anything.

What really bothered me about them was the way they would stand, with the prey wriggling in their bills, blinking stupidly out onto the world as if they didn't know what to do with the frog now that they'd caught it.

Anyway, Harry—if it was Harry—disliked human gazes as much as I disliked night heron gazes.

He flew up to the limb of an oak. I must admit the sudden flight was spectacular. Herons are powerful; a single flap gets them airborne, silently, effortlessly.

The Olmsted's Irregulars headed up the slope.

No one seemed to miss John Wu until we heard him yell out, "Wait! Wait!"

"Leave Harry alone!" Beatrice Plumb called out.

"I'm not looking at Harry anymore," he replied, without taking the binoculars from his eyes. "I'm looking," he declared, "at Abraham's binoculars."

We dropped everything. All binoculars went up to all eyes.

Yes. The braided yellow-and-black lanyard entwined around the thick, rotted limb of a long-dead beech tree was Abraham's.

We rushed over. The binoculars and the straps rested against the trunk of the live oak where the heron had rested. The oak grew at a forty-five-degree angle.

Harry flew away again.

Lucy climbed up the forty-five-degree angle like a lynx and pulled the sneakers triumphantly out of the cavity the binoculars had fallen out of.

We made a circle and gazed at the muddy junk upon the ground, after Lucy shook out the shredded Converse sneakers.

Our gaze was oddly reverential.

Like we were looking at religious artifacts buried long ago.

There was the pair of binoculars with the yellow-and-black strap.

There were the dismal, ripped high-top sneakers with two shoelaces on each.

There was a money clip with five twenties, two fives and three singles still intact.

There was a billfold with four credit cards, a driver's license, and various business cards.

There was a single leather glove.

There was a ring.

There was a notepad, spiral-bound.

There was a set of house keys on a ring.

"I never knew him to wear gloves," Beatrice noted.

"The key ring is the saddest, isn't it?" Peter Marin asked no one in particular. Then he added, "There are many rooms in the house of the Lord—but Abraham doesn't have the keys to any of them anymore."

It was a silly comment . . . but given the situation we all took it as some kind of spiritual truth and nodded our affirmation.

Lucy looked at her watch. "It is only nine o'clock in the morning. But we have surely done a full day's work. And we have made a startling discovery."

She wasn't talking about the warbler count. I knew that.

But to be quite honest, the only discovery we seemed to have made was that Abraham Lescalles had not been robbed, merely looted. And the loot had been hidden rather than taken.

But I did know that the only denizens of the park that hide loot are squirrels and drug addicts.

Chapter 4

Sometimes Lucy looks like a country bumpkin. Sometimes she looks like a sophisticated lady. Sometimes she looks like Lancelot's Guinevere. Sometimes she looks like an aging nymphet. Sometimes she looks like a mean librarian.

Oh, those are my derangements. After all, I am in love. Lucy looks like Lucy.

And she never looked more like Lucy and I never loved her more than when she strode into the NYPD Central Park Precinct that morning.

She was wearing a shawl.

And a flower print dress. Daisies.

And a red comb in her white hair.

And a single strand of pearls.

Tall and thin and willowy. Smiling.

With, of course, those horrendous birder boots of hers, which always made it seem that she was marching.

She said to the desk sergeant, whose name tag read Petrossian, "I would like to see your commanding officer."

The burly Petrossian just stared at her, then looked

at me and gave a little body-English move that seemed to ask me: Are you in charge of this woman?

I didn't say a word.

"Your commanding officer, young man," Lucy repeated.

"Well, lady, I—"

Lucy interrupted him vigorously. "Please don't call me 'lady.' My mother once had a deranged collie named Lady. She tormented chickens and children. Call me Lucy. Or call me Miss Wayles."

Petrossian didn't call her anything. He said, "I am afraid he is not available right now. Perhaps I can help you."

He now was looking nervously at the canvas laundry bag I was carrying, sailor-style, over my shoulder.

"Then," Lucy said, "I would appreciate it if you'd point me toward the officers who are investigating the murder of Abraham Lescalles.

"You mean the bird-watcher."

"Exactly."

He looked us over again.

"That would be Loach . . . Jim Loach. Why don't both of you take a seat over there and I'll try to get Detective Loach down to see you."

"Thank you," Lucy said.

We walked over to the rather severe wooden bench and sat down. And waited.

Ten minutes later a tall, stooped man with a beautifully bald head approached us. He said simply: "I'm Loach."

His weapon was prominent in a belt holster. He wore a dark shirt, a darker tie, and no jacket. He stuck his hands in the back of his belt and rocked on his heels.

"I'm Wayles," Lucy said, playing the game, "and this is Bloch," meaning me.

He nodded. We nodded.

Lucy said, "I have important information concerning the Lescalles murder."

Detective Loach pulled his hands around front and cracked some knuckles. He was interested.

"It was," Lucy announced, "definitely not what it seemed."

"What did it seem?" Loach asked, more puzzled than sarcastic.

"He was not robbed and murdered by two homeless men."

"Oh?" Loach asked, and then sat down at the empty end of the bench and crossed his legs. He looked, to me, like a weary chiropractor.

"Show him, Markus!" Lucy ordered.

I opened the laundry bag and shook all the objects out with a dramatic clatter.

"Damn!" Detective Loach said. He was off the bench like a cat, and kneeling beside the objects.

"So you see," Lucy said, "Abraham's murderer faked a robbery, looted the body, and stashed the objects on the far side of the pond. Then he left the murder weapon, a homemade knife, near the body. To implicate homeless people in the area. The facts of the case are now clear. Abraham Lescalles was murdered by a fellow bird-watcher."

"Would you mind very much," Detective Loach

asked, his voice dripping with sarcasm, "if we question the homeless suspects once we find them?"

"Not at all," Lucy replied benevolently.

Lucy took out her small spiral pad and started to write.

As she wrote, she said to Detective Loach, "I'm quite busy this time of year. But I will be home between seven and ten this evening and will await your call. We can discuss all the possibilities surrounding the case at that time. Markus and I have decided to give you and the NYPD all the help you need. Here is my number."

She handed him the slip of paper and out we marched.

She turned back at the door, suddenly, and called out, "Young man, I thought y'all are now supposed to be carrying 9-millimeter weapons. That thing in your holster is a .32, I believe."

Detective Loach stared blankly at her but didn't say a word.

"That poor man looks quite harried," Lucy whispered in my ear.

I arrived at her apartment a full twenty minutes before seven o'clock.

She had prepared meticulously. There were yellow legal-sized pads and sharpened pencils.

The phones, two of them, were on top of specially prepared piles of books.

Dipper found this setup intriguing. He used one of the book piles as a back-scratcher.

I didn't say anything, but her apartment looked like an old-fashioned horse parlor run by bookmakers.

She said, "I pulled out my second phone and plugged it in, Markus. So you can participate. I'm assuming this will be a conference call."

"Between whom?" I asked incredulously.

First she brought me a glass of cranberry juice. Then she answered.

"Well, I imagine Detective Loach will inform his commanding officer of our visit. And the commanding officer might well wish to consult with the borough commander. And he in turn might even contact the police commissioner."

My face must have registered confusion as to her expectations.

She patted my hand. "After all, Markus, it is a very high profile case and you and I are relatively unknown."

I must confess, the wait was quite pleasant.

Lucy, seated on the sofa beside me, waiting for the call, started reminiscing about books. I loved to listen to her. She would invariably start out: "Markus, I once read a book by an author whose name I forget. The title had the color red in it. It'll come to me soon. Anyway, it was a wonderful book. A novel. About a woman . . ."

That's the way she reminisced about books. And sooner or later she remembered the author, the title, and everything else.

At eight o'clock she fed Dipper. A half tin of economy cat food and a third of a tin of gourmet cat food. "He's on a diet," she explained.

At nine o'clock she decided to make some hamburgers.

At eleven o'clock she made two cups of tea.

At twenty minutes before midnight she picked up the phone and called the police precinct. Detective Loach was not there. There were no messages for her.

She smiled at me. "Have I been playing the fool, Markus?"

"No, Lucy. But it's like you said—we are relatively unknown. And we're civilians." Actually, she had been a fool to expect Detective Loach to consult her. And I was a bigger fool for not bringing her to her senses.

"Yes, yes," she said wearily. "I suppose you're right."

Then she said in a suddenly erupting Southern accent, "But the man dahd (died) in *mah* (my) aaahms (arms)."

Happily, she went back to middle English. "And *we* found his possessions. And he was *our* friend. And *we* are the ones who mourn him."

There was no response I could make. We sat in gloomy silence.

Finally, Lucy said, "I think I need a stroll, Markus, to clear my head."

I groaned. "But it's past midnight, Lucy."

She smiled. "Yes, so it is. Shall we go?"

I knew she could not be persuaded out of it. These "strolls" were an addiction of hers. And they were always at an hour at which no sane person prowls the streets of New York.

Moreover, Lucy was not afraid. I asked her often,

"Don't you believe the mugging and mayhem statistics?"

"No," she always said.

As for why she persisted with these strolls, here is a capsule explanation: Lucy believed that she had been a barn owl in a previous incarnation.

Now, barn owls hunt by night, and primarily by sound. And Lucy claimed that it was only at night that she could get a sense of the city. In the dark, all her senses bloomed. Because she was once a barn owl. My logical retort that she wasn't hunting mice fell on deaf ears.

Anyway, off we went on our stroll.

We walked north on Fifth Avenue. The night had turned chilly. And the moon had vanished.

Doormen peered at us through the doors. They were safe in their lighted lobbies.

When we reached Ninety-sixth Street, I tried to guide her east, but she kept heading north into the dicey neighborhood.

"The museum is closed," I whispered, trying to be funny. I was talking about the Museum of the City of New York, at 103rd and Fifth.

"Why are you whispering?" she demanded. "There isn't another soul on the street."

"Yes, they are here. You just can't see them, Lucy. The muggers are hiding, waiting to pounce on us."

"Shame on you, Markus. Frightened like this! A grown man who was born and raised in New York."

What could I say?

We kept walking.

Just as we crossed 101st Street, she stopped suddenly and grabbed my arm. Almost passionately.

"What is it?"

"I want you to know, Markus, that whatever it takes, I will bring the murderer of Abraham Lescalles to justice."

"Yes, I believe you, Lucy." Actually, I didn't, but discretion in these cases, to affirm the cliché, is always the better part of valor.

Her face was set in stone. She kept glaring at me.

"I believe you, Lucy."

"Even if the murderer is one of us," she added.

"You mean me?"

Her glare collapsed. She smiled and kissed me quickly on the cheek.

"But now, Markus, I have something else to tell you."

She took my arm, turned us around, and, to my relief, started heading back downtown.

"When that poor man was dying in my arms, Markus, I was experiencing a kind of revelation."

"About what, Lucy?"

"About healing the wounds. About compassion. About making an effort at reconciliation. Do you understand what I am saying, Markus?"

"Vaguely."

"I mean that it is time to heal the breach between the Central Park Bird-watchers and the Olmsted's Irregulars."

I stopped and stared at her.

It was an astonishing statement from the woman

who had actually orchestrated the schism. "Are you serious?" I asked.

"Quite serious. And you, my dear man, shall be the peacemaker."

I knew right there and then that I was in deep trouble.

She kissed me again on the cheek and said, all Southern wiles, "You're such a wonderful man."

Chapter 5

So I gave what could only be called a reconciliation party in my apartment. For all the members of Olmsted's Irregulars and all the members of the Central Park Bird-watchers.

The party commenced at four in the afternoon. And it was an immediate disaster.

I had purchased a great deal of prepared Italian food, champagne, and pastries.

In addition, I had rented a commercial coffee urn.

Yes, I was stocked. But not prepared.

Somehow I had forgotten all about plates, glasses, utensils.

So when the guests arrived they were forced to use the glasses and plates in my kitchen cabinets. Since I eat all my meals out, there wasn't much. People began to fight for glasses. It was getting ugly. Lucy was the one who went downstairs and came back with all kinds of paper cups and plates and plastic spoons.

"Everybody makes mistakes," she said to me, kindly.

Because this was the first party I had ever given, I really didn't know what to do.

I decided it was safest to assume my usual janitorial role.

I wandered about freshening drinks and disposing of empty plates and retrieving fallen napkins and sopping up little spills. I made the coffee. I monitored the bathroom. I changed the records.

As the party wore on, I lost my dourness. It was becoming fun. I even rolled up one rug and started to dance with Beatrice Plumb. It was a kind of lindy/tango.

As for Lucy, well, she was just wonderful in her party mode.

Every time I looked up she was with someone else, speaking and listening earnestly, bringing her message of compassion and reconciliation.

Maybe, I thought, giving parties should become a hobby of mine. It was obvious to me as the afternoon melded into evening that I was quite good at it. Maybe, I thought, I'll give parties twice a week, with increasingly sophisticated food and drink choices. After a few more paper cups of champagne, I could even visualize myself being contacted by the mayor to entertain distinguished visitors.

The last guest did not leave until past eleven.

It had turned out to be a very long party, and in spite of my janitorial efforts, my apartment was in shambles.

I collapsed in my father's easy chair, which had to be reupholstered every eighteen months.

Lucy sat across from me, on a straight-back chair with a cushion.

We both stared out the window toward the Hudson. The stars were actually twinkling.

"You did yourself proud, Markus. It was a grand party."

"Thank you."

"And the food was delicious. Those tiny smoked-salmon pizzas were scrumptious. Where did you get them, Markus?"

"On Ninth Avenue."

"My aunt Hattie always said that it takes a strong man to give a happy party."

I absolutely purred. I stretched out—tired, happy, and, admittedly, inebriated. This is what retirement is all about, I thought.

"Well, Lucy dear, did it work?" I asked, reaching for a cigar before remembering that I didn't smoke anymore and there were no cigars.

"Did what work?"

"The reconciliation. Are we now one happy group of bird-watchers again?"

"No."

I sat bolt upright.

"But . . . but I thought—"

She interrupted. "Aren't you happy in Olmsted's Irregulars?"

"Certainly I am," I replied, getting agitated. "But you told me that a reconciliation was in the works. You told me to give a party in order to make that happen."

"I really don't remember mentioning that, Markus."

"We were taking a walk on Fifth Avenue. And that's what you said!"

"Calm down, dear."

"I am calm!" I shouted. But then I realized I was standing up. So I sat back down.

"Why did I give the party, then?" I asked, an edge of testiness in my tone.

"You are getting upset, Markus."

"I'm not upset. I'm confused."

She got up and literally clapped her hands.

"I know what you need, Markus. Some card tricks to brighten your evening."

"Card tricks?"

Suddenly a deck of cards was thrust beneath my nose.

But they weren't playing cards. They were index cards.

Lucy flared them out in her hands.

"Pick a card, Markus. Any card."

By this time, I was so confused that I just reached out to pluck a card from the center of the deck.

"No. Not that one. The top one. And don't look at it."

I followed instructions. Maybe Lucy too had had too much champagne.

"Take another one."

Once again I started to select from the center.

And once again I was prevented from doing so, and guided to another card.

It happened one more time.

"Now, Markus, you have three cards in your hand."

"That appears to be true."

"Turn over the first one."

I turned it over.

There was a name printed in red ink on the upper left-hand side of the card.

The name was Jack Mowbray. He was a member of the Central Park Bird-watchers. He had been at the party. I knew Jack casually—he was a retired Con Edison manager.

"Turn over the second card."

I turned it. Printed on the card was the name Paula Fox. She, too, had been at the party, and was a member of the Central Park Bird-watchers. She was a widow.

"And now the third card."

I turned it over. Printed on it was the name of our own John Wu.

I looked up.

"What's the trick?" I asked.

"You've picked the killers, Markus. Congratulations."

"What?"

"One of those people, or perhaps more than one, murdered Abraham Lescalles that terrible day. One or perhaps more than one of those individuals was told about the eastern phoebe sighting by Abraham, lay in wait for him, murdered him, and disguised the scene to make it appear to be a bungled mugging by homeless people."

"You can't be serious, Lucy."

"Ah, but I am."

"But these are nice people! We know them!"

She just smiled at my comment.

"Why these three, Lucy? Why not any other three?"

"Aha! Let me explain."

"Please do."

"Did you see me talking to everyone at the party?"

"Yes."

"And did you notice that I spoke to everyone individually. In private."

"Yes."

"Well, Markus, I was making a proposal to them."

"What were you proposing?"

"Do you remember where we found Abraham?"

"Of course. Under that small bridge that leads to the Ramble."

"Right. Well, I proposed that we start a campaign to raise money for an Abraham Lescalles Memorial Fund."

"And just what is this fund for?"

"To rename that bridge in his honor, in his name. From the Bank Rock Bridge to the Abraham Lescalles Bridge. And put a beautiful carved memorial at the site of the murder. Maybe of an eastern phoebe or some other harbinger of spring."

"What does this have to do with anything?"

"Just listen, Markus. Virtually everyone thought the idea was ridiculous. For a variety of reasons. Some thought it was too elitist—after all, over the years, a lot of non-bird-watchers have been murdered in the Ramble. Why not name bridges after them? Oh, yes, Markus. There were many objections."

"So?"

"So, only three people were in favor of the idea: John Wu, Jack Mowbray, and Paula Fox."

"And what does that prove?"

"They were more than just in favor of it. They were enthusiastic."

"So?"

"So they are now prime suspects."

"How can you get from point A to point B? One doesn't follow from the other."

"Let me explain."

"Please do." It was getting to be a routine.

"Consider the blue jay, Markus."

"The blue jay?"

"Yes. The very wise blue jay. Tell me what happens when you approach its nest?"

"Well . . . I guess you're going to be attacked."

"Exactly. The jay comes at you in ferocious swoops and with a full repertoire of blue jay curse words."

I had no idea where this was leading. I just waited.

"Now, tell me where this attack will take place."

"Near the nest, I suppose."

"Wrong! A long way from the nest. The blue jay establishes its defense perimeter a long way from home. It launches preemptive strikes."

"Smart bird," I noted.

"Yes. And it would be equally smart for the murderer of Abraham Lescalles to encourage me to undertake a memorial campaign. It would be a kind of preemptive strike. Keep people thinking about the tragedy and therefore away from the nest . . . which in this case is the corpse itself. How and why he was murdered."

I must confess I was dazzled by how she had gone from point A to point B. I couldn't think of a refutation. So I made a suggestion.

"Why don't you give Detective Loach the names of your three suspects?"

"Don't be silly, Markus. Detective Loach obviously thinks I'm dotty. Perhaps even demented."

"What are you going to do, then?"

"You mean, what are *we* going to do, don't you?"

"Of course."

"We are going to find out who Abraham Lescalles was." Then her face brightened. "We are going on a field trip, Markus. Like Tinbergen. You *do* remember his great book on the herring gull, don't you? I gave you a copy to read."

"Yes, of course. A great book." I didn't remember whether I had read it or not.

"And we are going to create the same kind of life history for poor Abraham. His plumage. His courting and nesting habits. His grooming. His feeding. A true life history."

Even in my dazed and dopey state, I realized this was getting out of hand.

I grasped at a straw.

"I am still in shock," I said, "from what you said about John Wu. After all, he's one of us."

"What did I say about John?"

"That he's a suspect."

"Yes, he definitely is. He was almost crazily enthusiastic about the memorial idea. Don't you find that strange? John is a very cynical man—or so we thought. Yes, yes, yes, Markus. I have identified three suspects and John Wu is one of them."

"But it was John who found Abraham's possessions. Would a man who had hidden them disclose them?"

"If he knew I was looking for them. And he did know. What better way to preserve one's innocence? Yes, it was just another preemptive strike.

"Tomorrow morning, Markus. Bright and early. Same time, same place," she said, the latter phrase being the motto of Olmsted's Irregulars.

I fell asleep in the chair.

I dreamt that I was on trial for the murder of a herring gull.

I was just about to take the stand when a clanging in the kitchen woke me.

I sat up straight. Everything was dark. Where was Lucy? What time was it?

The illuminated clock said forty-one minutes past midnight.

I called out, "Lucy! What are you doing in the kitchen?"

The poor woman. She was doing the final party cleanup. Something I should have been doing. Rather than napping.

I hauled myself out of the chair and walked into the kitchen.

"Lucy," I said, "put the light on. It'll make it—"

I didn't finish. All the lights suddenly flicked on, temporarily blinding me.

I found myself staring at the blade and shaft of a knife.

The point was already against my naked neck.

I was absolutely catatonic with fright.

Then Lucy laughed and stepped back, pulling the knife away.

"I found this knife in your cabinet," she said.

She held it up in front of me.

"Does it look familiar?"

"No."

"Look at the blade, not the handle. Do you see? Two cutting edges. Regular blade on the bottom. Serrated blade on top. Like the blade of the homemade knife that murdered Abraham Lescalles."

"You have a point, Lucy."

"And there's something else," she said, holding the knife up toward the ceiling and rotating it in the light like it was an emerald.

"What? What?"

"I have seen this kind of blade somewhere else."

"Where?"

"I don't remember. Yet."

"Maybe you have one in your kitchen."

"Maybe," she said. Then she lowered the knife and caressed the side of my head as if I were a dog with a toothache. "What a long day this has been!" she added.

Amen.

Chapter 6

I arrived at the statue eleven minutes before seven o'clock. I was early.

Beatrice Plumb was already there.

"Sandpipers," she said, almost ecstatically.

"What?"

"Sandpipers, Markus, by Belvedere Lake."

"Ahh, sandpipers. Yes. That's terrific." I did like little shorebirds with long, skinny legs.

Peter Marin arrived next, then Lucy, then John Wu.

To each of them, Beatrice imparted her good news. The hunt, as they say, was on.

Lucy winked at me as we started out.

About a hundred yards up the horse path, Lucy made her move.

She fell down. And yelped.

"Lucy! Lucy!" I called and rushed to her side.

The entire commando group kneeled beside their stricken leader.

"Oh, it's just a sprain," Lucy called out.

I helped her up.

"Look," she said, "the rest of you continue the journey. Sandpipers are precious. Markus will take me home. I'll put some ice on it."

I could tell by the faces of the other Olmsted's Irregulars that they expected no less generous a response from their leader. The hunt was primary.

Off we hobbled, Lucy holding tightly onto my shoulder. Even though the whole thing was a scam, I felt gloriously relevant.

We hadn't gone more than ten feet when we heard a desperate shout. "Wait! Oh, please wait!"

At first I thought the shout came from the Olmsted's Irregulars.

But then the source became apparent.

Coming toward us was one of the most beautiful women I have ever seen.

She was tall and raven-haired, and she walked like a Parisian lady in an old black-and-white film—tapered hips swinging, taking small steps, as if her skirt were very tight and her heels so high.

But the truth was that she wasn't dressed in skirt and heels.

She was wearing one of those expensive jogging suits—this one was powder blue—and flat-heeled boots.

Around her neck was a tiny pair of opera glasses inlaid with mother of pearl.

"Hi!" she said, breathless, showing exquisite white teeth. She seemed confused as to which of the two groups to address—Lucy and me, or the bird-watchers just up the trail.

She finally decided on Lucy.

"I was at the boathouse and the bird-watchers there

told me you would let me tag along. They said you were a good group for beginners."

"We always welcome newcomers, dear," Lucy replied, not even getting upset by the insult.

Lucy called out to the others: "A new recruit."

Then she asked the young woman, "What is your name?"

"Emma Pip," the beauty answered.

Even from a distance I could see Peter Marin's eyes popping out of his head.

Miss Pip sashayed over to the embarking Olmsted's Irregulars.

"We are not used to such recruits," I said, trying to downplay the salacious tone that had crept into my voice.

"It is a pleasure to see some young people birding," agreed Lucy.

"Her youth is hardly her only asset," I replied.

"What do you mean by that, Markus?"

"I mean . . . ah . . . I mean that she is a lovely young lady."

"Are you sexually aroused, Dr. Bloch?"

I flushed. I felt that the wisest course was to let the question go unanswered.

We made our way out of the park, Lucy limping with every step, but the moment we stepped onto Fifth Avenue she discarded the hobble. Our ruse had not been detected.

Lucy pointed at the Church of the Heavenly Dove across the street.

"That is our first stop," she announced.

Then she added: "It is going to be a very long day. I want to prepare you for it."

"I'm prepared."

"This is going to be like pulling teeth," she noted.

"I'm prepared," I repeated, more emphatic this time.

"Good boy. You know you have a tendency to slack off, Markus. Perhaps it was your medical training."

"You're treating me like a malcontent," I said angrily.

"Calm down. The truth won't hurt you."

She took my hand and led me across the street.

We found the Episcopal priest affectionately called Father Rob in the alleyway between the cathedral and the administration building.

He was contemplating the pails used for recyclable garbage.

It took me a moment to realize that the man in the ragged sweater was the same bedecked priest who had presided at Abraham Lescalles's funeral service.

I liked him before he said a word. There was a fresh shaving cut on his chin. He looked like a dissolute Joel McCrea.

Lucy went right into her spiel . . . about how she was going to create a memorial for Abraham Lescalles in the park, right where he was murdered.

Father Rob listened politely and then replied, "Are you asking for my help?"

"Yes," Lucy admitted, "but it's not the kind of help you think. We're not asking you for a donation or anything."

"What then?"

"Your memories of Abraham, Father Rob. What he was like. What you remember of him. This kind of information will be most useful in our fund-raising."

Father Rob touched the shaving cut tenderly. Then he folded his arms and seemed to rock.

He finally said, "What can I say? Of course I knew him. But he was one of those men whom you seem to become friendly with, but there is no intimacy."

"Ah, then you were friendly with him?"

"Yes. I guess that would describe us—friends. I mean, we would have long conversations over coffee."

"About what?"

"Theology. Abraham was a very well read layman. We often took a walk together to the Paraclete."

"What is that?"

"It's that wonderful religious bookstore off Lexington Avenue. And afterwards we would go into a coffee shop and talk."

He stopped, smiled wistfully, and corrected himself. "No, not just talk—argue."

"About theology?"

"Well, the Markean Hypothesis."

"What's that?"

"Was Mark the first Gospel written?"

"Was it?"

"It was always thought to be. And Abraham believed it. Now there are questions. Some scholars have offered good evidence that it was the last Gospel. That is my position."

Lucy changed the subject. "Was Abraham ever married?"

"Not to my knowledge."

"But he did have women friends?"

"I don't know what you mean by that," Father Rob said, beginning to fidget a little.

Lucy pressed on. "That incident, Father Rob, in the church. Can you tell me about it?"

"What incident?" he asked defensively.

"You know what I mean."

"Yes, I suppose I do. And I'm weary of it."

"Please."

"Very well. It happened before I came to the parish. All I know is that they were found in the vestry. It must have been most embarrassing."

"Who was the young woman?"

"I don't know. She was married. She moved out to California soon after. But poor Abraham was, for many years, branded as a lecher, and worse." He smiled gently. "All that is ancient history. Let us only speak well of the dead."

For the first time, he looked at me instead of Lucy. I felt uncomfortable.

"Are you one of his bird-watching companions?" he asked.

"Yes," I replied.

"It seems fitting to me that the Church of the Heavenly Dove would have many birders among its parishioners."

Lucy didn't give me a chance to tell him I wasn't a parishioner.

She snapped her headband and asked: "Would you say, Father Rob, that Abraham Lescalles was a virtuous man?"

He looked at Lucy. "What an odd question."

"Yes, I suppose it is."

"Well, I am not in the business of judging virtue, Miss . . . uh . . ."

"Wayles," Lucy supplied, "but please call me Lucy."

"Thank you. Well, as to virtue, all I can say is this: Two days after Abraham was murdered, Mr. Nolan came to see me."

Lucy darted in. "Who is Mr. Nolan?"

"The doorman at the Hotel Winkler, the residence hotel where Abraham lived. Mr. Nolan was very distraught. He told me that Abraham Lescalles was the finest man he ever knew, and one of the most generous. He also told me that, after the murder, when the manager went to clean out the apartment that Abraham had occupied, he found almost no possessions. A few books, a few clothes, and nothing else. Abraham lived like a monk. And that, I suppose, is one form of virtue that no one would contest."

And that was the end of the interrogation.

"Where now?" I asked as we headed east on Ninety-first Street.

"To speak to Mr. Nolan," she replied.

"Too bad we couldn't get anything real out of Father Rob," I said.

"On the contrary, Markus. He was *illuminating*."

"I didn't hear anything important he said about Lescalles."

"Markus, how many times do I have to tell you? A worm that means survival for a robin is meaningless to a monkey eagle."

61

"Did your aunt Hattie say that?"

She didn't reply because the Hotel Winkler loomed up in front of us on Madison Avenue.

It was the last of the old Carnegie Hill residence hotels. No matter how many times they painted and renovated it, the aura of quiet desperation remained; it seemed almost to emanate from the bricks. The Winkler's clientele was extremely diverse—from well-off widows to starving opera singers to Taiwanese entrepreneurs. No children, however, were ever seen coming in or out.

Mr. Nolan was seated on an overstuffed sofa in the lobby.

He was wearing only half a doorman's outfit—hat and pants.

Mr. Nolan was a very small man with a beefy, lined face.

Lucy introduced herself and me. Then she said, "I don't know if you have been informed of the memorial fund for Abraham Lescalles. We wish to put a plaque in his honor in Central Park."

He put his paper down and shook his head. No, he hadn't heard.

"Mr. Nolan," Lucy declared, "I have heard that you were a good friend to poor Abraham, and we want you to speak at the ceremony."

Mr. Nolan flung his hands up in a gesture of protest. "I couldn't! I just couldn't!"

His eyes clouded over and the tears began to fall. Shamelessly, Lucy sat down beside him and comforted him.

"Yes," she said, "we all miss him terribly."

That sent Mr. Nolan on a further spiral of grief.

Finally, he got hold of himself. "I want to tell you what a wonderful man he was. Last year he got sick and he had to go to the hospital. It was night and raining. I started to help him out to the street to get a cab for him. He refused to call an ambulance.

"The moment we got outside and he saw it was raining, he demanded that I go back into the lobby so I wouldn't catch a cold. And he gave me a twenty-dollar bill."

Mr. Nolan threw up his hands in despair. "Oh, these homeless devils. These mad, crazed men. How could they have killed him?"

Someone at the desk called him. He walked away. Lucy folded her hands on her lap and regarded her grotesque birder boots with deep affection.

When Mr. Nolan returned he was more formal.

"Is there anything else I can do?" he asked, as if he owed Lucy something for refusing to speak at this nonexistent future event.

"Yes, Mr. Nolan. Any information you can give me about Abraham Lescalles will help me in fund-raising."

"What kind of information?"

"Well, hobbies, for example."

"Hobbies?"

"Did he have any special interests, any special friends?"

"He was active in that big Episcopalian church on Fifth Avenue."

"Anything else?"

"He went to the park every day to watch the birds."

"Yes, I know that. Anything else?"

"Not that I know of."

"Did he ever entertain visitors in his rooms?"

"Never."

"Did he ever go on vacation?"

"Yes. Once a year. For about a week."

"Where to?"

"I think down South. He went camping, on the Appalachian Trail. Or something like that. He always went to that big store downtown to get sleeping bags and flashlights and stuff like that."

"Did he drink, Mr. Nolan?"

"A bit."

Lucy sighed, closed her eyes for a moment, and then stood up and shook Mr. Nolan's hand.

"God bless," he said, and his eyes welled up again.

We walked outside. I had the strange feeling that Abraham was close by. My eyes darted back and forth, searching for that portly, kindly "pillar of the community" with his longish gray-black hair, blue eyes, baggy trousers, and inevitable cardigan.

We walked to the corner.

Suddenly Lucy embraced me.

"A treasure trove! Wasn't he, Markus?"

"What are you talking about, Lucy? He told us less about poor Abraham than Father Rob did."

She ignored me. "We are getting closer, Markus! Closer and closer. I feel like celebrating. I feel like making a jelly omelette!"

We headed toward Lucy's apartment, only two blocks away.

As we approached the house, we saw a well-dressed young man sitting on the stoop of the neighboring brownstone.

He was so well turned out that he might have been going to a job interview. And indeed there was an attaché case on his knees.

He stood up and asked, "Are you Lucy Wayles?"

"Yes."

"Hello. I'm J. J. Velasquez from the DOI."

"If you're J. J. Velasquez from the DOI, then I'm really L. L. Wayles from the OIBW," Lucy retorted.

Mr. Velasquez didn't know whether his nose was being tweaked or not.

"What does the J. J. stand for?" Lucy demanded.

"Nothing. That is my name."

"Not James or Joel or John—"

"Just J. J.," he replied.

"Well then, J. J., get on with it," Lucy demanded, laughing.

I wasn't laughing. I had suddenly realized what DOI stood for: the Department of Investigation of the City of New York.

"Perhaps we should discuss this elsewhere," young Mr. Velasquez suggested.

"Here will do just fine," Lucy said. "I don't allow strange young men in my apartment."

He shrugged. "Okay. I'll get to the point. As former director of the Archives of Urban Natural History, you are aware that half of its budget is paid for by New York City funds."

"I am aware of that."

"And I assume you are aware that the DOI is responsible for investigating any wrongdoing in organizations funded by the city."

"What wrongdoing? What are you talking about?" Lucy asked and promptly sat down on the stoop.

The handsome Mr. Velasquez whipped out a small notebook and started to read from it. "After you retired, Miss Wayles, the new director ordered a complete review of all the archives's holdings—including books, audio cassettes, videos, memoirs, manuscripts, and art portfolios.

"The inventory revealed that important assets were missing. To be precise: four watercolors by Harlow Trent."

Lucy's face showed her pain. I knew it was Lucy who had acquired the portfolio for the archives, at great expense. Trent provided the only real picture of the park at the turn of the century—the trees, birds, animals, and virtually every bridge and underpass.

J. J. Velasquez closed his little book. "Miss Wayles, do you have any knowledge of their whereabouts?"

"Are you accusing me of theft?" Lucy retorted.

"No."

"Malfeasance?"

"Of course not. We need your help."

"Well, Mr. J. J. Velasquez," Lucy stated dramatically, "as soon as I finish my current investigation, I will help you in yours."

A look of tremendous puzzlement crossed Mr. Velasquez's face then. Perhaps he was attempting to decide whether Lucy was completely innocent and had retired just as senile dementia was setting in, or whether she was the wiliest old crook he'd ever come across.

In any case, he stayed only a few minutes more.

"By the way," he called back to us after he'd taken ten or so steps away from the stoop, "what is the OIBW?"

"Olmsted's Irregular Bird-watchers."

He nodded. "Right."

He quickened his pace then, and soon disappeared from sight.

Lucy kept her seat on the stairs. She patted the step next to her. I sat down.

We were like two children sitting on the porch, waiting for the Good Humor man. In fact, I would have been pleased no end to see the anachronistic white truck rounding the corner, bells atinkle.

"What do you think happened to the watercolors?" I asked.

"They were probably just mislaid or misfiled. That's all. It happens all the time in a library."

"It used to happen in my laboratory also," I noted.

"That young man showed up at a most inconvenient time. I mean, just as we are about to solve the murder."

I stared at her, astonished.

"Didn't you know we are about to solve it? I was sure you knew."

I couldn't say a word.

"But first we have to go anting. Have you ever gone anting, Markus?"

"No. I don't know. Maybe. What is anting?" She was starting to confuse me greatly.

"Well, when crows, for example, get external parasites, they sit down on a live ant colony. The ants kill the parasites for them. Of course, it's a tad uncomfortable for the crows. But they get compensation. First, they get clean of parasites. Second, they get drunk on the chemicals released by the ants when they kill the parasites. Isn't that just a miracle, Markus?"

"Lucy, I don't have any external parasites."

"Then you're a man twice blessed."

"And I don't wish to get drunk."

Lucy took my hand in hers. "You dear man," she said, "we all have to make sacrifices. Don't you know that?"

And then she sent me home, a very confused man. My instructions were to meet her for breakfast the next morning. In Greenwich Village, of all places. For pancakes.

Chapter 7

The moment I entered the bakery the next morning, I remembered it from the past. No pancakes in this place.

I sat down with a cup of coffee and a blueberry muffin and waited glumly for Lucy.

Why had she wanted to meet me downtown, anyway? And if downtown, why La Guardia Place?

And why a place that didn't serve pancakes and never had?

Lucy showed up about twenty minutes late. The moment she slid into the seat opposite me, she dropped something white on the table.

I leaned over and looked.

It was a business card.

For one Lucy Wayles, President, Olmsted's Irregulars, Inc.

"Is this a joke?" I asked.

"No. I had them made up yesterday."

"We are not an incorporated bird-watching group."

"What they don't know won't hurt them."

"Who's 'they'?"

"The people I flashed the cards to yesterday," she

said. Then she took a bite of my muffin and a sip of my coffee.

She looked around. "Could you get me a light coffee, Markus? And a half a buttered roll."

"They don't sell half rolls, Lucy."

"Just coffee, then."

I got her the coffee.

"I told you I was going anting yesterday. Didn't I, Markus?"

"You did."

"Good. Well, after I picked up the cards, I went to the Paraclete bookstore."

"The store Father Rob mentioned?"

"Right."

"Why?"

She looked at me pityingly. I could tell she thought I must be awfully slow if I was asking that question.

Then: "So I entered the store and asked for the manager. She arrived. I handed her one of our new cards. She was suitably impressed. I told her that I represent hundreds—or did I say thousands?—of bird-watchers throughout the U.S. And that most of them are avid readers of bird books. Particularly bird books with religious themes."

She sipped her coffee and took another piece of my muffin.

"Is that true, Lucy?"

"Is what true?"

"That bird-watchers read religious bird books."

"Well . . . probably. I surely do."

"And then what happened?" I asked. I had no idea where this was leading.

"Then I glided into the trap. Ah, Markus, this investigation business turns one into a dissembler."

"You mean a liar."

"Don't be harsh, Markus. Let us keep our eyes on the prize."

"Which is?"

"Justice."

I pushed over to her the remains of the muffin. She devoured it in her lovely way.

"So I said to the manager that we are honoring three of our longtime members for service to the birding community. We want to provide them with memorable gifts from the bookstore. All three, I claimed, are good customers of her store, but we don't know their tastes in religious books. Could she go into her customer file and identify their last purchases from her store?"

"I take it that the three longtime members are the three suspects you identified for me."

"That's right. Jack Mowbray, Paula Fox, John Wu."

"Did the manager bite?"

"Not at first. She hemmed and hawed. She made excuses. She answered a phone call. But I waited on my perch. And finally she just went to her PC and started interrogating it . . . Markus, could I have another coffee?"

I got the coffee and a butter cookie.

"Only one of the names was on her customer list."

"Who?"

"Don't rush me, Markus. I made another stop."

"Where?"

"Do you remember what Mr. Nolan told us?"

"About what?"

"Abraham's hobby."

"Not really."

"He said that Abraham went camping once a year down South, and he outfitted himself at a big downtown store."

"Yes. Now I remember."

"There is only one big downtown store that specializes in camping supplies. It's on Park Row."

"So you went there?"

"Yes."

"And worked the same scam?"

"Please don't call it that!" Lucy retorted.

"Sorry," I mumbled, and broke off a piece of the butter cookie. Not the best, but not bad at all.

"But I did use the same procedure."

She leaned over and grasped my hand with excitement. "And, Markus, the results were the same. Only one of the three was a customer. *And it was the same one.*"

"Who?"

"Paula Fox."

"Well, good work, Lucy. But what does it mean?"

She sat back, smiled, and took a nibble of the cookie.

"It means that Paula Fox murdered Abraham Lescalles."

"Whoa! Whoa! Lucy . . . all it seems to me is that Paula Fox bought a book in a store that Abraham frequented. And bought a sleeping bag in a store that he frequented. It's sheer coincidence."

"Markus, there is no such thing as coincidence."

"What about motive?"

"Well, it is obvious that they were lovers."

"How do you know that? Just because they shopped in the same stores?" I was beginning to shout. I had to calm down. My eye suddenly caught a tray of napoleons on the counter. But it was much too early and it might upset Lucy.

"Get one if you want it," she said. She was very observant.

"I don't want one," I lied.

"Let us be logical, Markus," she said, patting my hand again.

"Yes. Let's."

"You will agree that Abraham was murdered either by a homeless man or a bird-watcher."

"I suppose so."

"And we now know it was not a homeless man."

"I suppose so."

"So it was a birder. And all evidence we have uncovered so far—circumstantial, of course—points to Paula Fox. Remember, Markus, if you leave your pet mouse in a locked room with an owl, and you return in an hour and the mouse is gone, you know that the owl swallowed poor Mr. Mouse. The evidence may be circumstantial, but the truth is plain. Even if you never find the remains of Mr. Mouse in an owl pellet."

I think I went into shock then. All kinds of images were dancing out of the remains of the butter cookie—owls, mice, pellets, foxes, Abraham's priests, doormen, knives, eastern phoebes.

Her question brought me back to the real world.

"Markus, why do you think I asked you to meet me here for breakfast?"

"I haven't the slightest idea."

She pulled out a map and unfolded it on the table.

"What is this?" I asked incredulously, securing the coffee, which had almost been knocked over.

"A street map of Manhattan," she said. She tapped a place on the map. "We are here, Markus."

I bent over. Yes, there was a cross on La Guardia Place.

"I know where we are, Lucy," I noted.

"Now look here. And here. And here."

I followed her finger as she tapped three other crosses surrounding the first one.

"Each of these crosses identifies the residence of a suspect. This place—this coffee shop—is equidistant to all three."

"So?"

"So? Are you asking me 'So?', Markus?"

"I am."

"Let me explain again. Here we are equidistant from all the suspects." She tapped one cross. "This is the only relevant one now. Paula Fox lives here. In Chelsea. On Seventeenth between Eighth and Ninth."

She plucked a napkin and folded it once, twice, thrice.

"Are you ready, Markus?" she asked.

"For what?"

"We will go to Paula Fox's residence. We will make a citizen's arrest for the murder of Abraham Lescalles."

I banged my hand on the table.

"This is the craziest thing I have ever heard," I shouted, and then brought my voice down to a desperate whisper. "You can't do this, Lucy."

"Why not? Paula Fox murdered Abraham. I am executing a citizen's arrest on her."

"This isn't the Wild West, Lucy. People don't do that anymore."

"People don't do a lot of things anymore. More's the pity. Shall we go?"

She folded up the map.

"Markus, did you hear me?"

"I'm not going, Lucy."

Lucy stood up violently, then eased herself back down. She looked very sad.

"It is very hard to believe, Markus," she said slowly, "that I have lived to see you abandon me."

"I'm not abandoning you, Lucy! Nor am I betraying you. I just won't do something that foolish."

"Tell me, dear. If my choice of action is foolish, what would be wise?"

"Jim Loach."

"Who?"

"The detective, Jim Loach. Go to him. Tell him what you found out."

"This is your *wise* choice, Markus?"

"I'm afraid it is."

"Detective Loach thinks we're both idiots."

"He may not think so after you tell him about Paula Fox."

"But, Markus, you think it's only a coincidence. Why wouldn't he?"

"Lucy, are you saying Jim Loach and I are interchangeable?"

Lucy began to laugh. I began to laugh. Suddenly all the bad feelings vanished.

"Perhaps," she said wistfully, "I was getting a bit dramatic with all those ideas of a citizen's arrest. As you have noticed and noted, Markus, I tend to go off the deep end."

How true! I thought. We had one more coffee and one more muffin. Then we headed uptown to see Detective Loach.

We finally found the detective at a crime scene. On West Drive, right by Tavern on the Green.

It was one of those peculiar Central Park crime scenes that happen only on nice spring days.

A rollerblader had been hit by a bicyclist. The cyclist had careened into a food cart. A kid had run off with the injured bicycle. The rollerblader had struck an EMS technician—actually kicked her. And the food vendor had suffered a kind of nervous breakdown; he was flinging frankfurters and knishes onto the road with furious swings of his arms.

We had to wait until the dust settled. Detective Loach seemed utterly contemptuous of the whole affair and he was mostly instructing a very young uniformed patrolwoman on procedures.

Finally, he started walking to his unmarked car, which had been parked in the Tavern on the Green lot.

Lucy and I pounced.

"Detective Loach," Lucy cried out. "How good to see you again."

He obviously had no memory of us.

"We had a conversation, Detective Loach, only a few days ago," she admonished.

Still no flicker.

"Concerning the circumstances surrounding the death of the bird-watcher, Abraham Lescalles."

"Oh, yeah," he said dully.

He played with the car keys in his hand.

"I have been conducting an investigation myself," she announced.

"That's nice," he replied.

She thrust an index card out to him. He took it gingerly.

"The woman whose name is on that card was, I believe, Abraham Lescalles's lover . . . and his murderer."

He studied the card. He looked at Lucy. He stared at me. Then he put it into his pocket and opened the car door.

"I'll look into it," he said.

"Her address is on the card."

"Yes, I know."

"I would suggest you take her into custody immediately," Lucy said.

Loach snapped back: "I told you, I'll look into it."

He slid into the seat. He put the key into the ignition. But he didn't start the car.

"Look, Miss Whatever-your-name-is, I appreciate what you did for us, finding the victim's property. But you ought to know one thing. There were two other assaults in the park that day. Both of them involved homeless perpetrators. In both, a knife was flashed.

And the description of the perpetrators in those robberies matched the description of the perpetrators in the Lescalles murder."

He waved the index card and added: "But I'll look into this."

Then he drove off.

Lucy and I walked slowly across the park and then uptown.

We exited the park at Ninetieth Street, in the shadow of the Church of the Heavenly Dove.

"I would like some wicked ice cream, Markus."

"What kind?"

"Make a suggestion."

"Vanilla fudge."

"Excellent."

I purchased the carton of vanilla fudge in a supermarket on Madison Avenue. Lucy preferred Breyers to Häagen-Dazs.

Then we repaired to her apartment, both tired, even though it was only twenty minutes past noon. The morning had been hectic.

Lucy placed the carton on a pile of books so that it would melt quickly.

On an adjoining pile of larger books, she placed two saucers, two tablespoons, and two napkins. She warned Dipper, who was draped over a bookcase, to restrain himself. The cat liked ice cream.

We sat down and waited.

"Do you really think that Detective Loach will look into the matter, as he says?" Lucy asked.

"Why wouldn't he?" I replied.

"Don't answer a question with a question, Markus."

"I don't know how else to answer it, Lucy."

The morning sun had vanished from her apartment. Everything was muted.

Lucy was calm, but I could sense her anger at me for aborting the citizen's arrest—it was there, hovering just beneath the surface.

I focused on the carton of vanilla fudge and tried to recall what I knew about Paula Fox. It wasn't much. A nice woman. A few pounds overweight. Not tall. Rather quiet. I remembered that she always wore sunglasses and had a purple knapsack slung over her shoulder when she birded. I couldn't remember anything that would lead me to believe that she and Abraham had been intimate in any way.

"Soon," Lucy said.

"Soon, what?"

"The vanilla fudge," she said.

I walked over to the carton and squeezed the sides.

"Not yet," I said.

For some reason, then, I found myself staring at the watercolor of the grotesque roseate spoonbill.

I had never seen one in the wild. Maybe the artist had exaggerated. But no matter how many times I stared at that likeness of the spoonbill, it was just plain ugly.

The plumage was pink and crimson. The head was naked, with an olive-gray bill that looked like an elongated carpet sweeper.

"Do you really like this bird?" I asked.

"Of course," Lucy replied tartly. "It's one of my heroes."

"This bird?"

"Yes. Unlike its cousins, the egret and the heron, the spoonbill does not hunt by sight. It's a head-swinger."

That made me laugh.

"It hunts by touch, sticking its bill into the water and swinging it from side to side. When it hits something juicy—snap goes the bill!" Lucy clapped her hands to illustrate the snapping shut of the bill.

"That doesn't strike me as a heroic hunting mode."

"It's more than heroic, Markus, it's painstaking."

Then she pointed to the ice cream carton, obviously wanting me to apply the squeeze test again.

I reached out.

The window . . . the left front window seemed to explode.

A thousand pieces of glass seemed to shower me.

I heard Lucy scream.

Then another window blew and something hard hit my shoulder and spun me around.

"Get on the floor, Lucy!" I yelled.

The world had turned to glass.

"They're shooting at us, Lucy!" I shouted. But I couldn't hear my own words.

Chapter 8

Actually, no one was shooting at us. And no one was trying to kill us.

We realized that about five minutes after the windows shattered. It took us about that long to get over the shock.

We were both on the floor, glass all around.

Lucy said, "Markus, is that your blood?"

There *was* blood on my shoulder. But it wasn't mine. It was from one of the objects that had been hurled through the windows and had struck me.

Two packages lay on the floor. Each one was about the size of the average best-selling book. Each was wrapped in newspaper and fastened with rope. And each was oozing blood from the corners.

"They frighten me," Lucy said.

I stood up, did a little dance to get all the glass off. Then helped her up.

"I must clean this mess up," Lucy said. But neither of us moved.

Then Dipper sauntered over, sniffed, ran his tongue over one of the edges, and sort of purred.

Lucy rushed over and gathered the big cat in her arms.

We kept staring at those malevolent bleeding packages.

"I'm going to open one," I said.

"What if . . ." Lucy stopped in the middle of the sentence, bringing one hand up to her mouth in horror.

"A head? Do you think they contain a human head?" I asked. Why were we being so silly?

I ripped open one of the packages.

Inside was about two pounds of raw calves' liver.

I ripped open the other one. Liver also.

"Stupid kids!" I said.

"What kids?"

"Neighborhood kids. Schoolkids. Maybe even kids from that private school around the corner."

"Do you really believe that?" Lucy asked.

"No," I replied guiltily.

"Tell me the truth, Markus. What do you believe?"

"That we are being warned."

She didn't answer for a while. She stared at the two shattered windows.

"Yes," she finally said, "I agree with you."

She dumped Dipper unceremoniously into the bathroom and shut the door.

Then she got a broom and began to clean up.

"What should I do with the liver?" I asked.

"Broil it, I suppose," she said. So I shoved the two packages into her freezer.

Lucy called the management company and reported the window-breaking.

"Should we call the police?" she asked.

"I don't see the point."

"Yes. I guess there is no point. But there is something I have to do that I can't seem to recall."

"You mean call someone?"

"No. I mean . . . ah . . . the ice cream, Markus."

I hurried to the container and squeezed the sides.

Perfect! I doled out the portions and we sat back down and ate the vanilla fudge.

It was a bit odd, staring out through the shattered windows.

"More, Lucy?"

"A trifle more."

I spooned some into her dish.

"Markus, I have been thinking."

"Yes, Lucy."

"I have been thinking about that funny cliché you always use. Or I guess it can be classified as a saying."

"Which one?"

"Oh, you know, the one about valor being ridiculous without discretion."

"That's not the saying, but it's close enough."

"Maybe it's time for us to step back. Maybe I should just write a short note to Detective Loach about this incident."

She finished the last spoonful before continuing.

"Then maybe I should take a few days of vacation. You know, my old friend Emily is sick. And I haven't been back to Chapel Hill in a long time."

"That sounds like a very good idea, Lucy."

*   *   *

And so Lucy went on vacation for a few days—to Chapel Hill, North Carolina.

And I stayed in New York and took a few days off from bird-watching.

The first day of her vacation I was fine.

The second day I began, early in the morning, to miss her. I mean, I really missed that woman. Love, of course, among us mature adults often gets out of hand. In my case, I became almost infantile, pacing and moaning.

Finally, to ease my pain and temporary loss, I decided on a therapeutic trip to the racetrack.

This was a mistake.

In the first race I bet on a horse named Ladybird. It lost.

In the second race I bet on a horse called Tarantula. It came in last.

In the third race I bet on two horses—Blue Bell and Antoinette. They came in fifth and seventh, respectively.

In the fourth race I bet on three horses. They all lost.

In the fifth race I bet on four horses. They all lost.

And then I realized that in the next race, the sixth race, I was about to bet on every horse in the race, just to get a winner.

Am I demented? I thought. Has love turned me into a complete and absolute ass?

I fled the racetrack immediately, went home, drank a bottle of wine, and fell asleep trying to read a history of Alexander the Great that purported to prove he died of alcoholism.

The next morning I ate a large, formal breakfast in a Greek luncheonette and decided to spend the day movie-going.

Alas, I only went to one movie. It was about a Latin drug gangster. In one hour and fifty-nine minutes, three people were disemboweled, two had their throats cut, one was beaten to death with a steam iron, and eleven were shot to death with handguns. There were only two rapes.

So I spent the afternoon at home contemplating a purchase of a new pair of shoes.

The phone range at 4:41. It was Lucy. Thank God.

"Markus," she said, "I understand you have abandoned the Olmsted's Irregulars."

Again that word—abandoned.

"No, Lucy. I just took a few days off. Anyway, how did you know?"

"Beatrice Plumb called me."

"How did she know where to get you?"

"I left my number with them—in case there was any trouble."

"When are you coming back?"

"Tomorrow."

"I'll pick you up at the airport. Give me the flight number."

"No. I'll take a cab. I'm going to go straight to the Archives and clear up that nonsense."

"What nonsense?"

"Markus, don't you remember J. J. From DOI? The missing portfolio? The Archives of Urban Natural History."

"Of course, of course."

"Good. Now, while I'm doing that, I'd like you to do something."

"What?"

"Beatrice Plumb told me that Peter Marin has gone around the bend."

"Oh, my. What happened?"

"That new birder. The young lady, Emma—Miss Tapp."

"No, Lucy. It's Emma Pip."

"Yes, well, poor Peter has fallen head over heels in love with her. He's smitten, but good. Perhaps even fatally smitten. I want you to go see him. Talk to him. Man to man, as they say. Make him see the light."

"I'll try my best."

"Good. That's that, then. Well, I'll see you tomorrow night."

"Wait, Lucy. How is your friend?"

"Not good. Good-bye."

"Wait! Lucy!"

"Yes?"

"How is the weather?"

"Glorious, of course."

"I miss you very much, Lucy."

"Go to the racetrack, Markus. Live a little."

And then she hung up.

Two hours later I was standing in front of Peter Marin's brownstone.

I buzzed for at least five minutes before the door opened.

Peter was absolutely naked except for his red bikini briefs.

In one hand he held what appeared to be a twenty-pound barbell.

"Well, look who's here!" he exclaimed. "Markus, how good to see you."

And, to my utter astonishment, he drew me to him with his one free hand and embraced me like a battle comrade back from a suicide mission.

Then he pulled me inside and slammed the door shut.

It was the first time I had ever set foot in Peter Marin's famous triplex on Seventy-ninth Street.

And it was an astonishing place. High and narrow like an oceangoing vessel, with spiral steel staircases.

"Where have you been keeping yourself, Markus?"

"Just resting."

"You missed some great action, you know. A solitary sandpiper. A pair of downy woodpeckers. A ruby-throated hummingbird. Laughing gulls. *And* a Philadelphia vireo."

I didn't get the chance to congratulate him.

Peter flung open a closet, stashed the dumbbell inside, and pulled out some clothes.

He slipped into powder blue sweatpants and sweatshirt.

"Let's go upstairs, Markus. I was just doing a little work. We can talk up there."

I realized I was staring at him.

It was the first time, I realized, I had ever seen Peter Marin in garments other than his Li'l Abner coveralls.

And there was something else.

My God! Of course! The man had gotten a haircut. His thick, unruly red hair was now stylishly coifed.

He even had half a part. And every one of his gray hairs had been tinted red. And the back of his cut had that popular shaggy-dog look.

"Well?"

"I didn't mean to stare, Peter."

"What do you think?"

"Nice."

"A hundred and thirty-five dollars, friend! Can you imagine that?"

We climbed into the work area.

"Here is where I earn my bread," he said, waving his arm to indicate the drafting tables, lights, special pens and pencils, compasses, and sundry unidentifiable objects in the room.

"What kind of campaign are you working on now? Perfume?" I had heard he did the artwork for some big cosmetic companies.

"Something special, Markus. Something very special," he whispered.

He made a motion with a hand to follow him. We climbed another staircase.

It was the bedroom. Just past the bedroom was a circular hallway, which wrapped around the entire circumference of this nautical triplex like a guardrail on a ship.

Peter flipped a switch and the walls were flooded with light.

I was astounded by what I saw.

Huge pieces of wrapping paper had been hung on the walls. Brown and thin.

And on each was a pastel fantasy, a kind of surrealistic combat between two figures. Or it might have been surrealistic lovemaking.

Whatever it was—the visual was staggering.

"Do you see? Do you see?"

"Yes, Peter, I see."

"Suddenly . . . what was it . . . two days ago? Suddenly my whole life became a sham. Suddenly I could do what I really wanted to do."

He walked to each panel and looked his work over.

"Do you understand what I am doing?" he asked.

But he didn't wait for an answer. "I am reinterpreting the great myth of Leda and the swan."

"You mean the Yeats poem?"

"No. The real myth behind the poem. Was it really Zeus who took the shape of a swan to make violent love to the beautiful Leda?"

"That's the way I heard it, Peter."

"And I say no! I say that Dionysius was Leda's lover."

"So, Peter, all these drawings are of the same myth?"

"Yes! Yes! And maybe a thousand more!" The bulky man was so excited his feet all but left the ground beneath them.

"You seem rather agitated, Peter."

"Not agitated, Markus. Stimulated! Alive! For the first time in years!"

My Lord. He had it bad. Fatally smitten. Lucy hadn't been far wrong.

But my instructions from Lucy were to deal with it man to man. What did that mean?

Not really knowing what to do, I just leaped ahead.

"How is that new young birder working out?"

"Emma?"

"Yes. I believe that was her name."

Peter grabbed my arm with such enthusiasm that I winced.

"She's incredible, Markus! She's breathed new life into all of us. Wait till you see her in action! Wait till Lucy sees her in action!"

I disengaged his arm. He was hurting me.

"She seemed to be a complete novice, though," I replied.

"Oh, no! Well, I mean, she's young, yes. But she has incredible sight. And incredible insight. And stamina. Oh, what an asset she is, Markus."

"No doubt."

"To tell you the truth . . ." Here, he paused and grabbed my arm again, then he asked, looking quite maniacal, "Do you really want to hear the truth?"

"Of course."

"She's our new heartbeat."

"What?"

"She's brought a new exciting heartbeat into our group. We pulse now! Do you understand, Markus? We're a living, throbbing, unified force now."

Whoa! I thought. This is much worse than Lucy knew.

"Can you be a little more specific, Peter?"

He threw up his hands in disgust at my insensitivity.

"You have to see for yourself. Will you be there tomorrow morning?"

"I can't. Lucy's coming back."

"Well, the next day, then. Wait! What is today, Markus?"

"Thursday."

"Okay. So you'll be back with us Monday. Then you'll see. And Lucy."

"I suppose so," I replied. The Olmsted's Irregulars never went birding on weekends. We left the park to the tourists on Saturday and Sunday.

Suddenly he looked at me in a confused manner.

"You're a doctor, Markus."

"So I am. Or rather, I was."

"You ought to know the significance of a heart-beat."

"I do, Peter. If you don't have one, you're dead."

"Precisely." He literally clapped his hands as if I had won the jackpot.

"I was dead, Markus. We were all dead."

I was about to ask what other miracles this Emma Pip could perform in addition to raising the dead. But I thought better of it.

I decided to change the subject.

"Do you know Paula Fox?" I asked.

Peter looked startled by my question, as if I had committed some kind of blasphemy by moving away from consideration of Emma Pip.

"Yes. I know her. But we don't see much of each other anymore. Ever since the split."

"What kind of woman is she?"

"I don't know. She seemed nice enough."

"Was she close to Abraham?"

"I don't know. Why are you asking these questions, Markus?"

"No reason in particular."

"Oh, yes, there is," he said bitterly. "I see what you're doing."

"What am I doing?"

"You're trying to tell me that Paula Fox is more my age. You're trying to fix me up with a woman my own age. Isn't that it, Markus? You're trying to show me what an old goat I am because I am responding to someone beautiful and young and exciting."

"No, I'm not! I don't care what you do with this Emma."

"Oh, Markus. I expected so much more from you," he said with genuine sadness.

He walked away. I heard him rummaging in a bin.

When he came back he was carrying a bottle of vodka.

I didn't know he drank.

He took the top off and drank deeply from the bottle.

Then he said, "Why should friends argue? You know what Baudelaire said!"

"No, I don't."

"He said—Stay drunk!"

"Ah, the French," was all I could reply.

I showed up at Lucy's apartment the following afternoon. She was there!

I had brought fifteen tiny yellow roses.

When I saw her my heart went flying.

God, I missed her. I grabbed her and kissed her and

held her so tightly that she cautioned: "Calm down, Markus. I was only gone a few days."

I stepped back and presented the bouquet.

She took it, curtsied, and went off to find a vase.

"Be a good boy and fill it," she said, presenting me with an empty milk bottle. I could tell she was in a strange mood.

But I followed orders. I filled the bottle, which originally contained chocolate milk that I myself had bought at the Fourteenth Street green market. An organic dairy farmer in upstate New York hawked his products there three times a week.

I plopped the roses into the vessel. They had seemed prettier in the wrapping paper.

The two blown-out windows, I saw, had been replaced already.

"Where should I put them?" I asked.

"I don't know. Find a place."

I placed the roses on a stack of books. I felt Dipper's eyes on me but I couldn't locate him.

"Look at that!" Lucy said bitterly.

"What?"

"The phone. See the answering machine? No calls while I was away. Not a single word from Detective Loach."

"Sad," I noted.

"Sad is not the word for it, Markus. This goes to the heart of the body politic. It disgusts."

She looked around—almost wildly. I had no idea what she was trying to locate, but she soon gave up the ghost. Lucy had returned home with a vengeance.

There wasn't a square foot of unoccupied space to be had.

"Do you know what, Markus? I am going to tell you something. I don't really know whether it was a youngster who broke my window or a shadowy conspirator trying to frighten me. And I don't really know whether my investigation of poor Abraham's murder has proceeded correctly."

She stopped. She stared at the phone machine. She shook her head.

"Markus, I am washing my hands of the whole thing. If the New York Police Department, in the person of Detective Jim Loach, does not think that my contribution is relevant, I don't want to participate any further."

"I agree, Lucy."

"Do you feel like eating?" she asked.

"Do you mean lunch?"

"Whatever."

"I could eat."

"Good. We'll go out. But first tell me about Peter. And then I'll tell you about my day."

"It's not good."

"Then Beatrice was right. The poor man is around the bend."

"Yes! First of all, he got this ridiculous haircut. Worse, he thinks he is re-creating the myth of Leda and the swan."

"What do you mean—re-creating?"

"I mean, he thinks he's Zeus and Emma Pip is Leda."

"My goodness!"

"And he is drawing a kind of massive wall painting featuring extreme forms of—how shall I put it?—avian pornography."

"Amazing."

"And he is drinking like a fish."

"Peter Marin drinking? That is hard to believe, Markus."

"Believe me. He was chugging it from the bottle."

"Did you reason with him, Markus? Man to man."

"I tried. But he wouldn't listen."

"Well, then, you know the next step, Markus."

"What, Lucy?"

"Speak to the young woman."

"You mean Miss Pip?"

"Now, who else would I mean, Markus?"

"But I don't know her. I don't even know where she lives."

"That's what telephone books are for. Find her. Call her. Visit her. Explain to her what is happening to poor Peter. She might not have an inkling. Do you understand, Markus?"

"Yes, Lucy."

"Now I want to tell you something . . . something so sad . . ." She threw up her hands as if she really couldn't deal with it. I saw her glance at the roses and then out the new windows.

"Is it Emily? In Chapel Hill?" I asked. Was that the content of her sadness? Was Emily dying?

"No. Listen, Markus. My plane landed at ten this morning. Then I took a cab to the Archives.

"I must tell you. I didn't get a friendly reception. Even from people who used to work for me. They

95

were very cold. They blame me for the trouble with the Department of Investigation. They blame me for the missing watercolors.

"But I found the ledger."

"What ledger?"

"It was a big book that everyone who used the Gold Room had to sign. Name. Item. Purpose. It was the Gold Room that held the Harlow Trent portfolios."

"Why is it called the Gold Room?"

"Because a Mr. Gold endowed it."

"Did you get the name of the borrower?"

"There are no borrowers. Archive material doesn't leave the building. But, yes, I found the name."

"Who?"

"Sylvia Rand."

"Do you know the name?"

"Yes."

"Who is she?"

"Oh, Markus, this is so sad."

"Why?"

"Sylvia Rand is Sheila Ott's sister."

"Our Sheila? The one who went crazy in the church?"

"Yes."

"Does she live with Sheila?"

"She doesn't live with anyone, Markus. She's dead. According to the ledger, she came to the Archives to view the portfolio on the first Monday in February— five years ago. She killed herself a week later. She had cancer."

"Why would anyone steal watercolors a week before committing suicide?"

"I have no idea."

"Why would a dying person want paintings by Harlow Trent? He wasn't a Picasso. He just painted Central Park."

"I have no idea."

"Are you going to call that DOI agent?"

"First I'm going to call Sheila Ott."

"What for?"

"Maybe she knows where the paintings are."

"How many were taken?"

"Four."

"What were they paintings of, specifically?"

"I don't know. The ledger had the numbers in the portfolio: fifteen, sixteen, seventeen, and twenty-one. There is no descriptive catalogue of Trent."

"It is sad, Lucy. The whole thing is sad."

She got up, walked to the mirror, and stared at herself.

"I am getting old, aren't I, Markus?"

"You look beautiful, Lucy."

"Will you go with me to see Sheila?"

"Yes. When?"

"Later on. After we eat."

"Let's celebrate, then. Let's have an opulent meal."

"Why?"

"Well . . . you're back . . . we're both alive. The windows are fixed. And you caught the thief."

Her face drained of color and I knew I had misspoken.

"Don't call that poor woman a thief!"

"I'm sorry, Lucy."

Her face suddenly exploded with radiance. "Oh,

those flowers you brought me! Look at them! How beautiful they are in the afternoon light. Did I thank you for them, Markus?"

I couldn't remember. So I didn't answer. Besides, I was getting hungry.

Chapter 9

The moment we stepped out of her apartment, Lucy became giddy.

"It's the plane," she explained. "There's a time lag. Eight hours after I step off the plane I become like a child again."

I chose one of those tiny, fancy new Italian restaurants that had been springing up like mushrooms.

By the time we sat down, Lucy had become nothing short of frisky. She refused to even look at the menu.

"I want something earthy," she said to the elegant young waiter. "I want an Anna Magnani dish. Meatballs and bitter rice."

"Anna Magnani wasn't in *Bitter Rice*," I said. "That was Sylvana Mangano."

"Then make it meatballs and very thin spaghetti."

"Would you like spaghetti Bolognese?" he asked.

"Spaghetti and meatballs."

It was really not the kind of place for that dish. It was like ordering pigs' knuckles at Lutèce.

But the waiter acquiesced, graciously.

I ordered a complex gnocci dish, which I couldn't understand at all.

We ordered a bottle of red wine.

The moment I filled the glasses, Lucy asked, "Are you ready for a toast, Markus?"

"Of course."

She raised her glass. I raised mine.

"To my brilliant but brief career as a homicide detective," she toasted.

We clinked and sipped.

She raised her glass again.

"And to what I hope is an equally brief career as a tracer of lost watercolors."

We clinked and drank again.

"And here's to Detective Loach. May he find the wisdom and tenacity to bring Abraham's murderer to justice. We must bear him no grudge."

She smiled. "Though the man is more than a little thick."

We clinked and drank again.

"And here's—"

"Shouldn't we slow down a little, Lucy?"

Her eyes narrowed.

"Markus, you're a kind, good man, but you can get somewhat preachy sometimes. Remember, I can outride you, outshoot you, and outdrink you."

Who was I to argue! I had never been on a horse in my life. The only gun I had ever fired was a BB gun. And after two vodkas I collapse.

She raised her glass again! "And here's to your new job as a mental health worker."

We clinked and sipped.

"Lucy, what are you talking about?"

"Well, I have charged you with the responsibility of getting Peter Marin under control."

"Oh, that. I don't think you can call that an exercise in restoring mental health."

"What, then?"

"I don't know."

"You can call it a case of reining in middle-age ardor. You'd be doing the man a kindness."

"He's in love, Lucy."

"That girl is young enough to be his granddaughter."

"She's not that young."

"Are you defending Peter? From what you and Beatrice tell me, he's making an ass of himself."

"Maybe she's encouraging him."

"You're going to find that out . . . aren't you, Markus?"

"I suppose so."

"Be firm with her, Markus. Explain to her that Olmsted's Irregulars are a very fragile bunch."

"Yes, I will."

"Good."

She put her glass down. I sighed happily. The waiter brought the food.

She picked up her utensils, paused, and asked, "What kind of coif did poor Peter get?"

"It's hard to describe. He has also started body-building."

"My, my."

She started to eat, then suddenly slammed the utensils down on the table.

"What's the matter?"

"Give me a quarter, Markus. I want to call Sheila Ott."

I gave her the quarter. She vanished down the stairway that led to the rest rooms and the pay telephone.

When she came back she said, "We're in luck. Sheila says to come over as soon as we finish eating."

"Where does she live?"

"On Central Park West."

"Did you tell her you wanted to talk about her sister?"

"I think I did, Markus. I think they were close. Sylvia was the older sister, if I remember correctly. Rand was her married name. They divorced a long time ago. I think there were two children—grown now, living in California. But I never knew her well. Then again, I don't know Sheila well, either."

"What kind of cancer?"

"Cervical, if I remember."

"You know what's strange, Lucy?"

"What?"

"That they both have names starting with an S."

"What's strange about that?"

"If I had two daughters, I just wouldn't name them Sheila and Sylvia."

"It's done all the time down home, Markus. There was a family that lived next to us who had seven children—all boys. Their names were John, Jake, James, Justin, Jesse, Jude, and Jeremiah."

"Why not Joseph?"

"Eat, Markus. Your food is getting cold."

I ate. She ate. The food was delicious. Lucy wanted

to leave immediately after the main dish but I persuaded her to have dessert and coffee, as did I.

It wasn't really the delicious Italian cheesecake I craved, it was staying there with her, then, in that place.

I was so comfortable and happy, in spite of all that had happened. She looked so lovely. White-haired, erect, fine-boned, with blue veins along her neck. I loved to watch her. There was something always going on on her face.

And her hands—playing with the stem of the wineglass. Her hands were like her face—plain and thin, but beautiful. Delicate but very strong.

"Tell me about Chapel Hill."

"What is there to tell?"

"Have things changed a lot?"

"Things always change. But it's still a college town. And a beautiful one, at that. Besides, I was there a few years back. Don't you remember, Markus?"

"No."

"Well, your memory is like a Swiss cheese lately."

"I think mosquito netting would be a better analogy, Lucy. Smaller holes."

She laughed. I laughed. But, as usual, the joy of being with her was being washed over by longing and frustration.

She wouldn't marry me. She wouldn't sleep with me. What was I supposed to do?

My self-pity turned quickly to self-loathing as I remembered Hawk Mountain.

I sipped my espresso and remembered bitterly, averting my eyes from Lucy's.

Lucy and I had gone to Hawk Mountain, in Pennsylvania, to watch the migrating raptors. It was late fall. The year before she found Dipper. We had two small rooms in a dingy horseshoe motel.

That first morning there was glorious. Sunrise. Cold. Wind. Soaring hawks. Excited people. Even I was enjoying myself. It was like a festival of hawks and falcons and eagles. Lucy breathed in my ear, "This is *the* fall migration."

We got back to the motel about ten and we retired to our respective rooms for a nap.

I was snoozing gently, fully clothed, on my bed, when I heard a knock on the door about eleven.

It was Lucy.

She was standing there with her coat open, and all she had on beneath the coat was a slip.

It was a blue slip. A beautiful slip with lace shoulder straps.

I saw her knees. This sounds strange, but it was the first time I had ever seen Lucy Wayles's knees.

I was struck by their absolute symmetry.

"I brewed you some home coffee," she said, her teeth chattering.

She came inside carrying two plastic cups and one of those small bottles of brandy.

She put the cups on the dresser, poured a smidgen of brandy in each, threw off her coat, and did a kind of swooning ballet step in her slip.

"Did you see them, Markus! Oh, those golden eagles!"

She spread out her arms and imitated the wind movement. Flap and glide. Flap and glide.

And then, before I could say another word, she flew into my arms.

That which I desired most was now within my grasp.

Thirty seconds later my beloved Lucy was in bed with me, naked in my arms.

And then disaster struck. To put it mildly, I couldn't function. Sexually.

The memory of that motel morning was so painful that whenever I dredge it up, something bad happens.

This time, I just dribbled espresso onto my shirt.

Lucy noted, "It is definitely time to go now, Markus. Before you drench your whole suit."

So we settled the bill and headed toward Sheila Ott's.

We were tipsy from all that toasting when we arrived at Sheila's.

But we didn't stay tipsy for long. Sheila Ott's apartment was so stunning it burned the wine away. Twenty-three floors up, with huge ceilings, and a terrace that seemed to hang in space.

You could stand there and see east across the park and then across the entire Manhattan Island.

For some reason, Sheila kept the apartment dark, except for one terrace light. But there was plenty of starlight flooding down onto the terrace and entering the apartment.

The first thing she showed us, somewhat sheepishly, was the high-power telescope she had installed on the terrace.

Alongside was a sturdy tile table on which lay pencils, notepads, and bird identification guides.

"I've been bird-watching from the terrace," she explained. "I'm just too ashamed to make an appearance in the park after I made such an ass of myself at Abraham's memorial service."

"That's nonsense, dear. No one remembers," Lucy retorted. "And even if they do remember, what of it? It was a heartfelt response, even if a bit excessive."

We all sat down on the cushioned wrought-iron swings.

It was chilly on the terrace and the breezes kept blowing, sometimes mildly, sometimes violently. I could see Lucy smiling. She liked heights. She liked the tops of buildings—where the hawks nested.

I found myself staring at that elegant mounted scope.

"I hope you're never tempted to become a Peeping Tom, Sheila," I said. "None of your neighbors will be safe."

Sheila laughed. "Sometimes I feel like Captain Hook scanning the sea for a ship to loot. When I told Paula about it, she went into a kind of shock."

"Paula?" Lucy interrupted. "You mean Paula Fox?"

"Yes."

Lucy gave me one of those quick, pregnant glances. Then she said to Sheila, "I didn't know you two were friends."

"We used to be very close. We still talk. She said that Abraham didn't approve of telescopes. She told me he once confessed that he longed to go birding without any binoculars; that he wanted the challenge of getting really close so he could identify the bird with his naked eye."

Suddenly she threw her arms up.

"Why am I babbling so much? Let me get you something. Tea? Coffee? Cookies? Drinks? Cold cuts? What?"

"Don't trouble yourself," Lucy said. "We just ate, Sheila."

"I'll have some ginger ale, if you have any," I said. The gnocci was beginning to make my stomach queasy.

"Three ginger ales it is," she announced, and slid open the glass door leading back into the apartment.

The moment she was out of sight, Lucy whispered to me, "Did you get the inflection in her voice, Markus?"

"No."

"I mean when she talked about Paula and Abraham. When she talked about Abraham's *naked* eye."

"I didn't hear any strange inflection."

"Yes. It was there. A catch in her voice."

She moved closer to me.

"Did it ever occur to you, Markus, that not only were Paula Fox and Abraham lovers, but also Sheila and Abraham. In fact, maybe all the bird-watchers in their group went to bed with Abraham Lescalles."

"I thought we had agreed to leave Abraham buried."

"I'm not digging him up. I'm just making a comment."

I tried to put some humor in the situation. "Besides,

if you start investigating again, you might discover that even you had an affair with Abraham."

"I don't have sex with preachers. You know what they say. Sleep with a preacher . . . sup with the devil."

"Since when was Abraham a preacher?"

"Well, he had that inclination, didn't he? A theological bent."

"You know, Lucy, I used to have a theological bent also."

"That's hard to believe."

"It's true," I affirmed. "When I got my first lab at Rockefeller Institute. When I first started studying cold viruses. Now, it dawned on me that here was this vast family of viruses, running from the benign to the positively deadly. And not one of them is good for you. If there was a God, I wondered, why hadn't he made at least one good cold virus."

"That was the extent of your theological bent?"

"I think I took it a few steps further, but I don't remember."

"You had too much wine, Markus."

At that moment Sheila returned with her tray. We each took a tall glass of ginger ale with a wedge of lime on the side. The glasses had been placed in holders with handles, like old-fashioned ice cream sodas.

So there we were, the three of us on the same swing, slowly swaying high above Manhattan.

Then Lucy said gently, "I want to talk to you about Sylvia." She took Sheila's hand into hers. I kept my eyes straight ahead. I had the feeling that I should leave—but I didn't.

Sheila didn't answer for a long time.

Finally, she said sadly, "You know, with my new telescope you can see exactly where she did it."

"The suicide?"

"Yes. In that parking lot by the boathouse. Early in the morning."

"The boathouse? Was your sister a bird-watcher?"

"Oh, no. I mean, I took her with me two or three times. But she wasn't interested."

"Did she make friends with any bird-watchers?"

"No, I don't think so. But she did discover that isolated parking lot."

Sheila suddenly put her glass down, brought her hands to her face, and uttered a low moan.

"Oh, God. I was implicated in it. I didn't want to be. But I was."

"What do you mean?" Lucy asked.

"The cancer was overwhelming her. She was getting sicker and sicker. Chemotherapy didn't work. Radiation didn't work. Nothing worked. She came to me and said she wanted to create one piece of good sculpture before she died. That was always my sister's ambition—to sculpt. She asked me to get materials—wood and metal and rubber tubing. But she never made that sculpture. She drove her car into the park and killed herself.

"She shot herself in the main artery of the neck. There was blood everywhere.

"She left a long note . . . a typewritten note Scotch-taped to the front window. She wrote that she couldn't stand the pain and the treatments anymore. And she couldn't stand the way she looked.

"My sister also thanked me for the sculpting material in the note and said she was just too weak to create anything more."

Sheila stopped speaking. She shook her shoulders as if someone had dropped ice cubes on them.

Then she said, very quietly, "When the police brought me the note to verify it, I had the terrible feeling that I was implicated in her suicide; that I never should have gotten the sculpting material for her; that it just held up a mirror to her plight and made her more depressed and suicidal."

Oh, it was a terrible story.

Sheila picked up her glass, left the swing, and began to walk around the terrace, quickly, as if she were trying to stuff those terrible memories back into a bottle. "At least you can understand now why I was so upset when it looked as though I'd played some unwitting part in Abraham's death, too."

"Of course I can," Lucy concurred, and then seamlessly switched gears by asking, "Did your sister ever shoplift?"

It was such an insensitive and intrusive question that all movement on the terrace seemed to stop—even the breathing, even the breeze.

But it was necessary, I realized.

"Why do you ask such a crazy question, Lucy? Of course she never shoplifted."

"Sheila, a short time before she died, your sister came into the Archives. She signed out a portfolio of a late-nineteenth-century watercolorist named Harlow Trent. When she returned the portfolio, four of the paintings were missing. She either misplaced them or took them. Do you know anything about it?"

"No! Nothing!"

"After she died, did you go through her belongings?"

"Of course. Her clothes. Her furniture. Her . . . everything. Most of it we sent to her children in California. The rest we gave to charity thrift shops."

"Did you find any paintings?"

"One or two. But I told you. She was a sculptor. At least that's what she longed to be. She had bought a few pieces over the years."

Lucy kept up her kindly, focused interrogation.

"They were watercolors of Central Park around the turn of the century."

"I told you. I found nothing like that in her belongings after she died."

"Sheila—tell me—think back. Is there any reason why your sister would have taken those watercolors?"

"No."

"Do you know why she would have wanted to look at them?"

"No."

Then I excused myself and stepped inside. I wasn't simply withdrawing to allow Lucy and Sheila a private moment. No. No, the sauce from the gnocci was punishing me.

When I came back, Sheila was showing off the finer points of her telescope to Lucy.

Five minutes later we settled into a cab on Central Park West.

"Isn't the whole thing strange, Markus?" Lucy asked.

"Inexplicable. But people dying of cancer do inexplicable things. Particularly if they're taking a lot of pharmaceuticals."

"Thank you, Markus. But tell me. Why didn't you say anything upstairs?"

"I just didn't have anything to say."

"You could have been more helpful."

The cab moved slowly south on Central Park West. I closed my eyes. What a long day it had been.

Then—without warning—"Stop! Stop!"

Lucy's screams almost burst my right eardrum.

The cab driver, a Sikh with a turban, braked hard. We were both thrown forward. Cars behind us began to honk.

"What? What is it, Lucy? What?" I asked as I bounced back against the seat.

Lucy had her hands over her ears.

The driver was glaring at me. I shrugged my shoulders.

"Markus," she ordered, "look out the window."

She pulled her hands from her ears.

"Are you looking?"

"Yes."

"What do you see?"

'A building."

'What building?"

"It appears to be the Historical Society of New York building."

"Yes! Yes!" she yelled, and then kissed me.

She began to laugh.

"This aging is terrible, isn't it, Markus? We are getting old. Our memories are going."

The Sikh kept glaring.

"Be calm, Lucy. What are you talking about?"

"I completely forgot that the Historical Society of New York has slides of Harlow Trent's work. If I can't find out why Sylvia Rand stole the watercolors and I can't find out where they are now, at least I can find out which ones she stole. What numbers fifteen, sixteen, seventeen, and twenty-one look like."

I looked out the window again.

"Drive on," she ordered the driver.

To me, she said: "We can go there tomorrow afternoon. I have an old friend who works there. Help is on the way!"

She tapped my shoulder.

"But you have a task to perform before you accompany me. Don't you, Markus?"

"Task, dear?"

"The name of the task is Emma Pip."

I had forgotten all about Emma and Peter Marin. It must have been the gnocci.

Chapter 10

Usually on Sunday mornings I laze in bed. Sometimes I even think. Sometimes I fantasize about the future—where Lucy and I will be living after we get married. If, that is, she ever consents before we are both in the grave.

But that Sunday I was like a percolator. I had to find Emma Pip, who was not listed in the white pages or with Information.

It took calls to Peter and Beatrice and Lucy, who in turn made other calls, until there was a telephone dragnet out by bird-watchers just to get me to Emma.

Finally, after all the raw data was analyzed, I was told that Emma Pip would be in the coffee bar on Greene Street and Houston, in Soho, at approximately eleven a.m.

In fact, I was informed, Emma Pip was there every Sunday morning about eleven.

I took a cab downtown. The coffee shop was enormous, one of the new kinds, situated in what had once been a gallery. Indeed, the owners of the place still mounted small exhibitions on the walls.

I ordered a mug of mocha with whipped cream, a blueberry square, and a glass of water with ice.

The bill was ridiculously high for such a modest repast, but the items were so tastefully arranged on the sturdy bamboo tray that I didn't really mind.

With tray in hand, I wandered into the main seating area.

I spotted Emma Pip immediately. She was seated at a back table, directly under the skylight.

Once again she was wearing a jogging suit. But this one was rose-colored. The top was unzipped and beneath it was a black ribbed polo shirt.

She was reading a book.

Her face was a kind of mournful mask—beautiful, serene, mysterious. Most truly beautiful women share a strange quality: It is as if the face has been painted by an artist rather than built by genetic combinations.

As I approached, I could see that she was reading *Peregrine.*

That unnerved me.

What the hell was a novice bird-watcher doing reading the ultimate birder's cult classic?

When Lucy had given me her copy to read, she had warned me that if anything happened to the book she would torture me to death.

Had Peter Marin already entrusted his copy to Emma Pip? If so, the poor man might be beyond help.

I must confess, it was the only bird book that absorbed me totally.

Published in the 1970s and long out of print, it is the real-life diary of a man called Baker.

This Baker, who lives in the west of England, becomes obsessed with a peregrine falcon.

He leaves home and hearth to follow the falcon.

At the end of the book, he has become so absorbed by the lifestyle of the bird that he and the falcon fight over a duck the peregrine has killed.

"May I sit down?" I asked politely.

She looked up from her book. For a moment, she hadn't the foggiest idea who I was.

Then her beautiful face lit up. She put the book aside.

"What a wonderful surprise, Dr. Bloch."

"Markus. Please call me Markus."

It was a good omen that, although we had met only once, she remembered my name.

"Do you live nearby?" she asked once I was seated.

"No. Uptown."

I stirred my coffee, then sipped it.

She cradled her face in her hands and watched me.

"The coffee is good here, isn't it?"

"Yes," I agreed.

"Why haven't you been to the park lately?" she asked.

"Busy," I said.

"And Lucy Wayles hasn't been there either," she noted.

"No, she hasn't. But Peter has kept us informed."

"Oh! Isn't he great!"

"Yes. Great."

I ate a small piece of my blueberry square. This wasn't going to be easy, I realized. Not at all.

I picked up her book.

"Have you read it?" she asked.

"Twice," I lied. Then my lie astonished me. What was the point of it?

"What does Lucy Wayles think of it?" Emma asked, and she leaned over expectantly, as if Lucy's words were Gospel.

"Oh, she loves it. It was her copy I read. Lucy says there are three great bird books. One is *Peregrine*. The other is Tinbergen's *The Herring Gull*. And the third is *The Falconer of Central Park*."

"I never heard of that one."

"It was also written by an Englishman. A reporter living in New York who spent all his time bird-watching and people-watching in Central Park."

She laughed her beautiful laugh. It was infectious.

Then she said, "I heard there were more kinds of birds and more kinds of people in Central Park than any other similar space of ground."

"Probably so."

"I mean on the planet!"

"Why not the planet?" I responded, and finished off the blueberry square. For some reason I was sweating.

"Do you think she'll write a book?"

"Who?"

"Lucy."

"About what?"

"About birds."

"I don't know. It never occurred to me. She never said anything about a book."

"But she's the most famous bird-watcher in the city."

"Lucy? Famous?"

"Of course. That's how I got into bird-watching, Dr. Bloch. I mean, Markus. When I saw her on television. She was so brave. Climbing that icy bridge to rescue the gull."

"It wasn't a gull," I corrected. "It was a duck, a tufted duck." Beware the tufted duck, I quoted Lucy silently.

She threw back her arms. "How wonderful it must be to bird-watch with her! What an adventure!"

I sipped my coffee, trying to stop my eyes from following the curves of her willowy body, trying to make them turn away from that ribbed polo shirt beneath the sleek jogging suit.

It was time, I realized, to speak the truth.

"Emma, I did not really come here by accident. I came to find you!"

She leaned forward in anticipation.

"Why? Did I do something wrong?"

"Not really, Emma, but . . ."

I stopped midsentence and began moving my cup like it was a chess piece. This was going to be very difficult.

"Well, you are a beautiful woman," I said.

"Thank you, Markus."

"A beautiful *young* woman."

"I'm not a teenager."

"Of course not. I meant—I think what I am saying is . . ."

Then I got totally confused. Get to the damn point, Markus, I said to myself.

"I'm here to talk to you about Peter Marin."

"Oh!"

"He is beginning to act very peculiarly. We are all worried about him."

"What is he doing?"

I glared at her. Was it really possible that she didn't know—that she hadn't picked up on it?

"Come now, Emma. The man is making a fool of himself. He's head over heels in love with a woman almost forty years younger. With you."

She shook her head from side to side.

"Believe me, Markus, I had no idea."

"And even worse, he thinks you're in love with him."

She shook her head again. "I like him. I admire him. But the reality is—"

"Reality isn't the problem. His fantasy is the problem, Emma."

"What do you want me to do?"

"I don't know."

"I can't very well stop talking to him."

"Well, we have to think of something."

We were both silent for a long time. The coffee shop was so cavernous, I felt that I was in an airline terminal waiting for a connection.

"Maybe," she said finally, "I do bear some responsibility."

"You said something to him?"

"No. No. Not that. It's just that I have always been attracted to older men. Always."

"Why?"

"I don't know. To be honest with you, Markus, the only thing that has kept me from having an affair with an older man is that they have lost their taste for adventure. And I love adventurous men. Explorers. Pilots. Even, sometimes, criminals."

I laughed.

"Our bones hurt too much for adventure," I said.

She suddenly reached across the table and covered one of my hands with one of hers.

I was startled.

"Please don't make fun of me, Markus."

"Believe me, I'm not," I replied, pulling my hand away on the pretense of wanting to drink from my cup. Of course it was empty.

She sat up straight. Like she had made some kind of decision.

"Okay. I shall try to distance myself from him," she announced.

"Good."

"I'll try to control all my enthusiasms while I'm birding with the Olmsted's Irregulars."

"Good."

She stood up. "I have to go."

I smiled at her. I held out my hand. She took it quickly and then dropped it.

She began walking toward the exit. She stopped. She took one long stride back to me and quickly and warmly kissed me on the cheek. She smelled of wildflowers.

I sat in that coffee shop for a long time after she left.

Mainly because my damn legs were trembling.

Five hours later I was seated next to Lucy in a coffee shop on Seventy-second and Columbus.

It was a prearranged meeting and we were both on time.

This time I ordered an imported cherry soda with a spectacular fizz.

Lucy had lemon cake and water.

Since it was Sunday, the construction crews who were ripping up the avenue were absent. But we could see clearly the pilings and the equipment. In fact, it was almost all one could see.

Lucy seemed in good spirits. She was wearing a peasant blouse of yellow silk with a black vest with silver buttons. She looked like a Hungarian freedom fighter. When she turned her head and the afternoon sun hit her white hair, she looked like the first woman preacher to ascend the pulpit in Fairfax, Virginia, or maybe Fayetteville, North Carolina.

Lucy always set me to speculating.

"Well, get on with it, Markus," she said.

At first I thought she meant my fizzy soda.

But then I realized she was inquiring about my meeting with Emma Pip.

"It took a while," I said.

"To do what?"

"To get her to understand Peter's condition. And the cause of his condition."

"And the denouement, Markus?"

"The what?"

"Denouement. Tell me the end of the story. Good Lord! What's the matter with you, Markus?"

"Nothing's the matter with me. It just wasn't an easy assignment."

She patted me encouragingly on the wrist, which I resented.

"Proceed at your own pace," she said.

"It took her a while to understand. She claimed that she really wasn't flirting with him."

"Something must have happened to turn Peter into the village idiot," Lucy said.

"Well, when I finally persuaded her of Peter's sad mental state and his bizarre pattern of behavior . . . when I finally, after much explanation"—this was an exaggeration—"made her understand that Peter was desperately, hopelessly, ridiculously in love with her . . . she said . . ."

And here I paused, but not for dramatic effect. Simply because I had forgotten what exactly she had said.

Lucy fidgeted impatiently.

"Oh, yes. Distance. She said she would 'distance' herself from him."

"Excellent, Markus."

"Thank you."

I finished my soda.

"And now to the next matter at hand," Lucy announced.

She studied her watch.

"We have to be there in about thirty-five minutes. Davey is waiting for us. The slides will be all set up."

"Has he worked at the Historical Society for a long time?"

"Since before you were born, Markus. And he's not a he. Davey is a she."

"Funny name for a she."

"Her full name is Davida. What should she be called—Lefty?"

"There's no need to get angry, Lucy."

"I didn't mean to snap at you. But let's get down to business. Davey is an old friend of mine. Professionally, she's a whiz. Personally, she's—oh, let's just say she's something of an eccentric. So I must warn you: There is a good possibility she will try to provoke you. Just don't respond."

"I'll try not to."

"She can be difficult. She's a smoker. And when smoking was banned from all public buildings, she refused to step all the way outside the building to smoke. She kept one foot in and one foot out. It was her protest against the ban. The administration threatened to fire her. She took them to court. She once even sued a visitor to one of the galleries because he told a child accompanying him that one of the eighteenth-century portraits was a fake."

"Strange lady," I commented.

"And she doesn't like birds or bird-watchers."

"And she's a friend of yours?"

"There are many rooms in the house of the Lord, Markus. But, yes, Davey can be trying. She used to proudly announce that in her opinion birds are merely rodents who grew feathers and wings because they were too incompetent to survive on the ground. A bird, in her view, is a flying rat."

"An unfortunate term."

"Yes, it is. But Davey has her good points."

"I'm sure she has."

Off we went to the Historical Society, which was

located in a beautiful landmark building on Central Park West.

We waited, inside, near the small gift shop, for about ten minutes. And then Davey Plomer burst upon the scene.

She was a large black woman with some kind of arthritic condition that gave her shoulders and arms a batlike quality. She was wearing a painter's smock over her dress.

Lucy and she greeted each other as if they were the survivors of a shipwreck, meeting again after twenty years. Although it was obvious they had just talked on the phone. How else could they have set up the slide show?

Then Lucy introduced me. Davey stepped back and looked me over, with some distaste evident.

"I've heard of you," she said, and then she ignored me completely.

"Listen, Lucy. There is something you must know."

"What?"

"Remember when we were closed for renovations?"

"Yes. For about eight months."

"Well, during the renovations a hidden cellar was uncovered right in this building."

She pointed down toward the floor dramatically.

"Right below us, I believe. And do you know what was found there?"

Lucy didn't know. Nor did I.

"Old cannonballs. And kegs of powder. And blasting caps. They're still there. This building could go up at any time."

It was becoming obvious to me that Lucy had understated the case when she described Davey as something of an eccentric.

"And there's one other important thing you must know. A gentleman was here asking questions about you and Harlow Trent, the watercolorist."

"Oh. You mean that young man—J. J. something. From the DOI."

"Yes. Lucy, he believes that you took the missing items. He believes it!"

"Young men are peculiar."

"Amen to that. But I'd sue him. For defamation of character."

"Not to mention alienation of affection," Lucy added, and then gave me a quick glance.

We headed toward the slide room single file.

It was a small refurbished room with lockers, folding chairs stacked along the walls, and a slide projector on a ledge.

A screen had been set up against one wall.

"Get some chairs," Davey said. I opened two folding chairs. Lucy and I sat.

Davey flicked the wall light switch. Darkness.

"Slide one," Davey announced. "Number seventeen in the Harlow Trent portfolio."

The image appeared on the screen.

It was a lovely winter park scene.

Two riders on prancing horses were on the bridle path, heading under one of the park's bridges.

The time of day appears to be late afternoon, and the snowflakes are large and soft.

"Beautiful," Lucy noted.

"They don't make paintings like that anymore," Davey called out.

"It's the Daleheed Arch. Right near Tavern on the Green," Lucy said, identifying the bridge.

"Next?" Davey called out.

"Please."

"Number eighteen," Davey announced.

This was an early spring scene in the park. Again on the bridle path.

A horse has obviously just thrown a rider and is nibbling spring shoots happily. The rider, a young woman in an elegant riding outfit, is shaking her crop angrily at the horse.

In the background is a very small bridge.

"That's Riftstone Arch," Lucy said. "It's a famous bridge. No bricks or mortar. Just plain old stone—Manhattan schist. I think it's one of Calvert Vaux's best."

"It's across from the Dakota apartments," Davey added.

"Next!"

Another slide.

A soft summer meadow beside what Lucy identified as the Eaglevale Bridge, right across the street from the Historical Society building, just inside the park.

I recognized it. "That's near the Balcony Bridge," I called out happily, "where we stop for a rest and a bite all the time."

"Correct," Lucy said, affirming my geographical literacy.

"Yeah," Davey called out mockingly. "That's where you weirdos roast and eat those sad little creatures."

"Next slide, please," Lucy called out, not rising to the bait.

The final slide showed a watercolor of an old man with a top hat and a cane on one of the cast-iron bridges linking the Reservoir footpaths to the main drive. A storm is coming. The sky is threatening. A few crows are hovering.

Then Davey shut off the projector and switched on the light.

"I'll tell you, Lucy, all this makes no sense at all."

"You might be right."

"It isn't my field, but I know a thing or two about Harlow Trent. I know he's not a famous artist. I know that five or six of his works are now in postcards. But they're his Christmas watercolors. About Christmas in Central Park, when everybody was happy and pink-cheeked and carried ice skates on their shoulder."

"I agree," I said happily. And then shriveled when Davey glared at me. It was obvious I was supposed to be seen but not heard.

"Did you make stats of the slides for me?" Lucy asked.

"They're being made now. I'll send them over."

"Thank you."

"And remember what I said about J. J. Whatshis-name."

"I will. I'll see my lawyer in the morning."

Everyone laughed.

As we left, Davey called out, "The pigeons in the park are now transmitting Asiatic flu."

"I'll be careful," Lucy called back.

Once outside the Historical Society building, Lucy said, "Let's take a walk to Lincoln Center."

"Why?"

"I want to see the fountain."

So we walked there, slowly, in the late afternoon light, actually holding hands. Lucy was very quiet. I realized that the visit to Davey had been a major disappointment to her. If she had thought to find some clue in the slides as to the watercolors' disappearance, she was now not a whit wiser.

It was obvious to me that our investigation into the stolen watercolors was going to go the way of our investigation into the murder of Abraham.

And that was fine with me.

When we reached Lincoln Center, Lucy said, "I want to sit up close to the fountain, so I can feel the spray."

So we sat right down on the edge, along with the young lovers, music students, eccentric seniors, and others who always seemed to ring the fountain.

The Sunday afternoon performances were breaking and people streamed out of the buildings.

"Why don't you ever take me to a concert?" Lucy asked suddenly.

"You never ask to go."

For some reason she found my simple response very funny.

"Would you like an ice cream?" I asked, noticing the small ice cream booth set up in front of the concert hall.

"Vanilla," she said.

I left the fountain and returned with two cups of vanilla ice cream.

"Why do you always order the same ice cream I order, Markus?"

"Because it doesn't matter to me—the flavor. I like all ice cream. So it's the easiest way."

"I don't understand that."

"All I have to say to order is 'two vanillas.' Rather than 'one vanilla and one strawberry.'"

"There must be one ice cream you don't like."

"There might be."

"Of course there is. I remember distinctly. Yes—boysenberry."

"Okay. You're right."

"So, if I told you I wanted a cup of boysenberry ice cream, you wouldn't order two boysenberries."

"No, I guess not. But why are we getting into a fight over a stupid ice cream?"

She looked up innocently. "Fighting? I didn't know we were fighting. I thought we were having a discussion. I am beginning to notice, Markus, that native New Yorkers tend to look upon all discussions as fights."

She finished the ice cream and crumpled the cup. I finished mine. I took both cups and put them into the receptacle.

We sat by the fountain without speaking. Just watching the incredible tableau of people.

We sat there for a very long time. I wondered how long she wanted to sit there. Lucy is usually on the go most of the time.

When darkness started to fall, I asked, "Lucy, do you want something to eat?"

"No, thank you. Markus, I've met someone."

"Someone I know?"

"No. I've met someone with whom I've fallen in love. I can't see you anymore."

"You *are* joking, aren't you?"

"No."

"Ah, I see. This is some kind of test. Like boysenberry ice cream."

"No. No test, Markus."

I stared at her. The realization was slowly growing that she was quite serious.

Then I got so frightened that I kissed her on the cheek.

"Stop that!"

I pulled away.

"There's only one way to do this, Markus. I'm very sorry. You are the most splendid man I know. But I've met someone else. I love him. I have to make a sharp break with you. I have to end it. Now. Here. It's the only way."

And then the full reality hit me. I felt every ounce of strength leave my body. I could hardly keep from toppling over. I could see myself crumpled on the ground.

"It is the only way, dear Markus," she whispered.

"Who is this man you have met?" I croaked.

"What does it matter?"

Then I fairly shouted, "Because I want to know his name."

"His name is Duke."

Duke? Was he a baseball player? Like my old idol, Duke Snider of the Brooklyn Dodgers. No! It couldn't be *that* Duke.

"Where did you meet him?"

"At the museum."

"What museum?"

"What does it matter?"

"Is he tall?"

"Not really."

"Does he smoke? Does he drink? Does he send you flowers? Does he have money? Does he wear shoes with laces? Is he a Republican? Does he read?"

I started asking questions like a crazy man. Nonsense questions. I couldn't stop, until I was exhausted.

Then Lucy took a handkerchief from her purse and carefully patted my brow.

"You're sweating, Markus. You'll catch a chill."

I batted her hand away. She stood up quickly.

"It could never work between us, Markus."

"We never tried!" I yelled.

And the people around us began to move away, suspicious.

She started to walk away.

"Let me call you tomorrow, Lucy."

She shook her head no, almost violently.

She started to walk faster.

"Lucy! Lucy, please!"

But she was walking down the steps, toward Broadway.

And then I couldn't see her at all.

Chapter 11

Thus began those dark days . . . the days without Lucy.

Who would believe that a mature, enlightened physician (albeit nonpracticing) and scientific researcher (albeit retired) would be ensnared in such a snare?

Me! A devoted admirer of the Stoics and Voltaire and Spinoza. Me! A man who prided himself on Reason.

Obviously I crumpled quickly.

When I got home that evening, I fell onto my bed, fully clothed, and slept until the next morning, when the alarm woke me.

I got up wondering what I was doing in my clothes.

I showered and dressed as usual, preparatory to leaving for Central Park and the Olmsted's Irregulars.

At 6:40, just as I was about to leave my apartment, my memory returned.

Had it really happened? Had it been a dream?

I called Lucy. The moment she heard my voice, she hung up the phone.

I waited five minutes and called again.

She hung up the phone again.

I sat down on the bed.

Lucy was out of my world.

For the longest time I sat there, trying to understand exactly what that meant. Then, I tried to make toast. The slices burned. I spilled the corn flakes. I dropped the milk.

So I sat back down. And I felt a sense of aloneness that was so thick I could scarcely breathe.

Afterward came self-loathing. Lucy left me with just cause—I was a vile creature. Vile! Ugly! Fat! Without a single redeeming trait.

Without honor. Without virtue. Without goals or aspirations or allegiances.

I lay down.

Then came a murderous rage—against myself and Lucy and the world.

I jumped up and flung a shoe across the room. It hit nothing.

You must calm down, I cautioned myself.

I was still enough of a doctor to remember that aloneness, murderous rage, and self-loathing were the three signs of impending suicide in a mature male.

A letter. It was obvious a letter had to be written to Lucy.

I wrote thirty-one pages' worth—a rambling letter that begged, threatened, and covered every emotion under the sun.

Then I ripped it up.

Then I took another shower and banged my head severely on the shower head.

And that was the first day without Lucy.

On the second day, I knew I had to get out . . . do things.

I went to the zoo. I went to a movie. I went to Bloomingdale's and bought two pairs of pajamas.

I went to the Jefferson Market, in the Village, and bought olives and tomatoes and halvah.

That was the end of the second day.

On the morning of the third day, I sat up in bed and listened to a music program that was paying tribute to Dinah Washington, playing some of her greatest hits.

The songs became too sad. I snapped off the radio.

Oh, Lucy! I began to weep. Uncontrollably.

On the fourth day, I took a ride on a train up to Albany. I walked around for about five minutes, then went back to the station and waited for the next train back to New York.

On the fifth day, I took a bus to Atlantic City and lost $275 playing blackjack.

On the sixth day, I purchased a boxed paperback edition of Proust's *Remembrance of Things Past.* Or is it . . . *Times Lost?* I read three pages from the third volume and shoved it into my closet with the shoes.

On the morning of the eighth day, I woke up and had a kind of revelation.

I needed a friend. I needed someone to talk to.

And more than that, I needed someone to tell me, Markus, you are wonderful.

I needed a woman.

Not Lucy. Not anymore. But *some* woman. I needed any woman.

A name . . . a face . . . a figure kept popping up. But I kept pushing it down.

Up it popped. And then I couldn't bury it.

Emma Pip.

Was I mad? I was even older than Peter Marin.

She had kissed me. But what did it mean? She had said she liked older men. But she had also said she liked adventurous men.

What was going on here?

Would I become an idiot like Peter? In ludicrous love? Lifting weights. Getting coifed.

I hurried to the mirror. Nothing would help me.

Oh, Lucy! Why did you leave me? This was terrible.

I rushed out of the apartment to take a long walk.

As I walked I kept looking for May-September couples.

There were plenty of them.

But what was the context? Were they father and daughter? Were they boss and assistant? Were they teacher and student?

Or were they lovers?

It didn't matter. Each sighting made me feel better . . . made me more confident.

I bought a cigar. My first in years. I took it home like a giddy schoolkid and smoked it to the bitter end.

If Lucy could see me now, I thought with a kind of perverse triumph.

Would Emma Pip entertain a relationship with me?

Not in my current state.

But what if I were an adventurer? Would that entice her? What a combination! A much older man living on the dangerous edge.

Maybe that was her fantasy.

The problem was, I realized—and it was a severe problem—how could I masquerade as an adventurer?

Skydiving in New Jersey?

Becoming a secret agent? A drug lord?

Smuggling computer chips out of Hong Kong?

Currency manipulation out of an office in Singapore?

Gunrunning along the Mexican border?

All of these were out of character.

I began to laugh derisively at my nonsense. Even if I were the reincarnation of the Scarlet Pimpernel, Emma Pip would probably want nothing to do with me.

Suddenly I grew very fatigued. I lay down. Older men and fantasies are a bad mix.

As I lay there, I tried to remember just how many days it had been since I'd seen Lucy. Sometimes it seemed like only minutes ago, sometimes months ago.

She was probably with that Duke now. Whoever he was.

Every day that passed . . . every moment made the whole thing more unbelievable to me.

Lucy never said she wasn't happy with me!

It had come out of the blue.

Obviously I had done something very wrong. Obviously I had done something or said something or behaved in a manner that she could no longer tolerate.

Oh, Lucy! What have I done? Why won't you forgive me?

And who was this Duke?

It was no use, I realized. All this second guessing. All this attempt at reconstruction.

I would never know the real reason Lucy Wayles dumped me, because I would probably never see her again. Never.

That thought, right then, numbed me to such an extent that I lay catatonic on my bed for hours.

From time to time I had peculiar dreams or visions or hallucinations.

Lucy transforming herself into a great horned owl and flying off with a mouse in her beak.

Lucy, absolutely naked, on a rock in the center of the ocean. Chained. Her hair so long it fell into the water.

Lucy, in judicial robes and huge horn-rimmed glasses, banging her gavel down and sentencing me to all kinds of horrific punishments.

Lucy, in her coffin, so pale, so still, so white. Holding in her arms a bunch of lilacs and a framed photograph of me.

That last image undoubtedly signaled the end of my nervous breakdown.

I remember that I got up, ordered in several Thai dishes from a restaurant on Fifty-eighth Street, consumed them down to the last drop of peanut and coconut oil, then went to sleep again.

I was awakened by wailing sirens. Police? Fire! EMS?

It didn't matter. All seemed okay. I was calm. I was clear-headed.

Is this the moment when grief ends? I thought.

Suddenly the sirens ceased. I got out of bed and walked to the window.

One EMS truck and two patrol cars were in front of the building across the street.

What was going on? A domestic dispute? A heart-attack victim?

I watched and waited.

Someone was wheeled out on a gurney. The EMS loaded him. The truck drove off. The police remained, making notes in their pads.

They were probably taking the victim to the emergency room at Roosevelt Hospital, only three blocks away.

I wondered what emergency room Abraham Lescalles had visited.

How the hell did that pop into my head? I thought.

Ah! For some reason of crossed synapses, the poor man across the street reminded me of what that doorman at Abraham's hotel had told us . . . how Abraham had fallen ill one evening and taken a cab to the hospital. And how, even while sick, Abraham seemed more worried about the doorman getting out of the rain than his own discomfort.

I walked away from the window. But I couldn't walk away from the connection.

I took a banana, peeled it, and sat down gingerly on the bed.

My mind had begun to race in peculiar ways. Nefarious ways. A scenario was forming in my head . . . a scenario that would rescue one fool from loneliness and despair.

What if I really were a private investigator . . . conducting an investigation into the murder of Abraham Lescalles?

Of course, I had already helped Lucy in such an investigation. One that had ended without resolution.

What if I used the fact that I was *Doctor* Markus Bloch to investigate Abraham Lescalles's "illness"?

What would it matter? Lucy wouldn't care. She had washed her hands of it. And she would never find out.

It wouldn't hurt the police investigation. After all, whatever illness drove Abraham to a hospital that night had been marginal. He had lived and recovered. Only to be murdered months later.

It would be a meaningless adventure.

Except to Emma.

Oh, this was the hook I was looking for. A secret life. She could accompany me on my investigation. She could . . .

Whoa! I had to slow down. My brow was feverish.

I started thinking of objections. But they were all trivial. It would be a harmless adventure—for the dead and the living.

Suddenly I would be transformed into a mysterious adventurer . . . a man who lived on the edge of danger. Emma would find me irresistible.

That slowed me down even more. If she did find me irresistible, there would be another problem. A very private problem.

It had been a long, long time since I'd been with a woman. A very long time.

And that debacle with Lucy in the motel room pointed out the dilemma.

A young woman would expect a much older man to be an expert lover. No doubt about that.

I shoved the stump of the cigar into my mouth and started to pace.

Books wouldn't help at my age. Or videos. It was obvious what I needed. A refresher course.

I needed a lady of the night.

You can imagine my state of mind at the time, that not only did I consider it a rational course, but I acted on it.

The clock read 2:00 A.M.

I dressed carefully and walked out onto Fifty-seventh Street.

Of course a streetwalker was not plausible, social diseases being what they were.

Nor did a massage parlor seem inviting.

No. It had to be a high-class call girl. I would just explain to her the situation, pay the fee, however exorbitant, and get a refresher course.

I headed toward the nearby Carlson Hotel on Seventh Avenue. Having lived in the neighborhood for many years, I had heard rumors that the doormen at the Carlson routinely supply call girls for tourists.

I waited across the street to get my courage up.

The doorman on duty was in a resplendent outfit. A young man, heavily built, with a florid face, he was pacing between the door and the curb.

The night was balmy. A lot of people were still

walking, most of them returning to the many hotels in the area.

Twice, thinking of Lucy, I lost my courage and headed back toward my apartment.

But each time I reconsidered, and finally I crossed over and walked up to the doorman.

He looked through me.

"Good evening," I said.

"Right," he replied.

"I live in the neighborhood," I said.

"That's nice."

"On Fifty-seventh Street."

He opened the door for a guest.

"I need your services," I said.

"You want a room?"

"No."

He sighed. "What do you want, mister?"

"I need a woman."

"Is that so?"

"A good woman."

"Don't we all?"

"Just for the night. And I will pay well."

He narrowed his eyes. "You a vice cop?"

"Of course not. Do I look like a vice cop? Aren't I a bit too old?"

"You might be a bit too old for a lot of things."

I ignored the insult. "Can you help me?"

"I'm a doorman, not a pimp."

"Yes, I know. But—"

"Get lost."

So I crawled back to my apartment, totally deflated.

I decided to forget about the whole business. To consign myself to loneliness.

But the next morning, when I got up and planted my feet on the floor, and realized that I was facing another day without Lucy, I knew that, come Sunday, I would show up at that coffee shop on Greene Street, at about the same time that Emma Pip arrived.

Or perhaps just a few minutes later.

Sunday. I dressed a trifle garishly, a trifle arrogantly.

I walked a few blocks downtown, practicing a kind of swagger—then took a cab.

My heart was pumping on the ride down and the back of my shirt was damp from sweat.

It is tough being a lonely adventurer on the make.

I wanted to look like Jean Paul Belmondo, but I was afraid I looked more like Chevalier.

Emma was there! At the same table.

But this time I didn't order a blueberry square. Just black coffee.

She straightened right up when she saw me.

"Oh! Lucy told us. About the breakup. I'm really sorry, Markus."

I sat down and shrugged dramatically.

"How's the old bird-watching?" I asked, with just a little catch of contempt in my voice.

She started to talk a blue streak, about the birds they had seen. About Lucy. About Gertrude. About Peter Marin and John Wu.

I wasn't really listening. I was watching her. She

was so young and so beautiful and so vibrant that she seemed a different species altogether.

"Don't you miss it, Markus?" she asked.

She was wearing the rose-colored jogging suit again. With a white ribbed polo shirt under it this time.

"Some," I said, smiling, then added mysteriously, "But right now I'm after bigger game than warblers."

She leaned forward, excited. "What?"

I made a gesture with my hand signifying that I couldn't say any more about it.

She nodded and sipped her coffee.

"How is Peter? " I asked.

"I think he's better. I tried to do what you suggested. Distance myself a little. The first day he was very grumpy. But now he seems fine."

"Good."

I wanted to ask her about Lucy. But I couldn't. The whole situation was too peculiar. She seemed about to say something concerning Lucy, but kept quiet.

I sensed that she had picked up something new in my demeanor . . . something different . . . perhaps something exciting.

I leaned forward and gestured with my hand for her to lean forward also.

"Can I trust you, Emma?"

"Of course."

"I mean *really* trust you."

"Yes, Markus. Believe me."

"All right. I'll tell you what I'm doing." I sipped my coffee. "Do you remember Abraham Lescalles?"

"I never met him. I heard what happened, though. I heard about the murder."

She was interested now. Very interested. I could see the future. She and I together. On walks. In theaters. Even bird-watching, if she wanted. I could see us shopping together. I closed my eyes for just a moment. Had she really kissed me? What kind of kiss had it been?

"I'm on the trail of his murderer."

She exhaled. "But the police!"

"Forget the police!" I whispered savagely. Then I waited twenty seconds. "If you are not afraid of danger, Emma, I can use your help."

She rolled her beautiful eyes and leaned forward across the table. "I crave danger, Markus."

"Are you sure?"

"Yes."

"Do you crave danger . . . tonight?"

"Tonight?"

"Yes. Tonight is a crucial night in the investigation. Hard, dangerous legwork."

"Count on me, Markus."

I wrote my address on the paper napkin. "Be at my apartment a little before midnight."

"What shall I wear?"

"What you have on is fine."

"Will we have weapons, Markus?"

Right then I wondered if maybe this whole thing was getting out of hand. But it was too late to go back. Hello, happiness! Good-bye, loneliness!

"Not on us, Emma. But they'll be close by."

She smiled knowingly.

I slid out of the coffee shop like the adventurer I was.

An hour before Emma was supposed to arrive, I gave Lucy another chance.

I called her.

She hung up the phone.

I called her again, begging for a hearing.

She hung up the phone.

A hard-hearted woman.

There was nothing else for me to do but proceed with the plan.

Emma arrived twenty minutes before midnight. She was wearing a charcoal gray jogging suit with a scarlet chiffon scarf at her neck. It took one's breath away.

I unfolded a map in front of her, just as Lucy had unfolded a similar map in front of me, in that downtown coffee shop.

"What's this?" she asked in her lioness voice.

I pointed out where Abraham had lived. And then with a sweep of the hand indicated the locations of the possible emergency rooms he had visited that night.

"He went to either Lenox Hill, Metropolitan, or New York Hospital," I announced.

She nodded. As if I had uttered a profundity. Yes. She was clearly excited.

"My instinct tells me it's Lenox Hill," I said, trying to sound like Leslie Howard, "but we'll be thorough and try them all."

She nodded. As if my analytical ability were beyond reproach. Then I had to sit down for a moment.

Away from her. Because I was suddenly overwhelmed by the closeness. After all, I'm not a young man. And all this was new to me. Oh, Markus! Thou lecherous heart!

We were facing one another across the table.

Her eyes were wide with the excitement of the coming chase.

Then she made that movement with her hand, pulling back her luxurious hair. Her face betrayed a stab of confusion.

"Markus."

"Yes." I reached out and touched her hand. Oh, Lucy! Forgive me! You forced me to do this.

"What does it mean?"

"What does what mean, Emma?"

"That he went to an emergency room in a hospital?"

"It's crucial," I lied. I began to get nervous.

"It could have been a mere stomachache."

"Possible. But doubtful."

"I mean . . . what does it have to do with his murder? I understand he was murdered by homeless men in the park. A long time after."

Uh-oh. She was getting to the heart of the scam.

I had a sudden urge to confess . . . that she was right . . . that it was just a way to seduce her . . . to get her to think of me as an eligible adventurer.

I wanted to shout: "Of course there's no connection between his murder and his visit to an emergency ward . . . a trivial occurrence recounted by a doorman. He might never have even gone to a hospital. He might have taken his medicine at the nearest bar instead."

But all I said was, "Trust me."

"Oh, I do! I do!"

I relaxed. But my leg was throbbing. I was not alone. I basked in the camaraderie. Good-bye, loneliness.

"But Markus, how do we get the information? Do we just walk in? And will they have a record of his visit? If he did visit."

"All emergency rooms keep detailed, updated patient databases. They have to. For medical insurers. And for the lawyers."

"Lawyers?"

"One of the commonest forms of malpractice suits deals with intake practices in emergency rooms in hospitals. You live or die there, my dear."

"But why will they give you that information? You're not the police."

"I have credentials," I said.

Then I whipped the badge out of my picket and placed it on the table.

She leaned forward and read the wording on the plastic identification badge, which I had saved from the last AAAS convention I had attended.

MARKUS BLOCH, M.D., PH.D.
PROFESSOR OF MOLECULAR GENETICS
ROCKEFELLER UNIVERSITY, NY, NY

"Wow!" she said.

I pressed on with my papier-mâché adventure.

"Having established my credentials," I continued, "I will then provide a rationale as to why I need the information immediately. I will tell them that my friend Abraham Lescalles is a medical researcher, that he is working in South Africa, and that he was struck down and is currently in critical condition in a hospital in Cape Town."

"But Lescalles is dead," she interrupted.

"What they don't know won't hurt them. Besides, the information I want in order to possibly save his life is simple and basic: Was he treated there? Diagnosis? Treatment?"

"Why are we going to the hospital after midnight? Why not during the day?"

"Simple. Because at that hour there is no administrative staff. The desk nurse handles the intake computer. There won't be time for so much red tape."

"That is brilliantly underhanded," she said admiringly.

"Are you ready, my dear?"

"Yes!"

"We'll go to Roosevelt Hospital first. It's only a few blocks from here."

She rose like a beautiful feline. Little did she know that I planned Roosevelt Hospital to be my first and last stop. Then I would toss the whole adventurer nonsense over and invite her for a drink in some darkened cocktail lounge, where Sinatra was the only choice on the jukebox and it is perpetually quarter to three in the morning.

We went downstairs, the security guard in my building eyeing me suspiciously. He had seen Lucy here on many occasions. But this creature on my arm was not Lucy.

We walked uptown toward Roosevelt. It was such a lovely night that I took a somewhat circuitous route.

There were few people on the street. Sunday night/Monday morning is quiet in midtown west.

Suddenly she stopped short.

I looked at her inquiringly.

She threw her arms around me.

I was so astonished I almost fell down.

"Make believe we are lovers embracing," she whispered in my ear.

"Why?"

"We are being followed! We have been followed since we left your apartment."

"Are you sure?"

"Yes! Look past me. Can you see anyone?"

All I could see was a white-coated hospital attendant snatching a smoke.

She disengaged herself.

We walked into the hospital—an odd couple indeed.

It was astonishing how smoothly the plan unfolded. The desk nurse was visibly impressed by my badge. She listened to my story of woe concerning Abraham Lescalles dying in a Cape Town hospital because of a mysterious disease.

She punched his name into the computer. No Abraham Lescalles had utilized that emergency room.

We walked out.

"This is turning me on," Emma purred.

Yes. She was right. It had been exciting.

"Where next?"

"The Plaza," I said, initiating part two of my plan.

"What hospital is that?"

"It's a hotel. And there's a bar on the Fifty-eighth Street side that serves the best littleneck clams in the city. I thought we could go there . . . and have a drink . . . and relax."

"But what about the investigation?"

"We can continue it some other night."

"But you can't do that!" she said anxiously.

It began to dawn on me that I might have created a monster.

"Besides, alcohol will dim our faculties," she added.

"And the clams might induce hepatitis."

"Yes. Yes. Oh, Markus, let's go on. This is fun."

It also dawned on me that I should have figured a backup if part two of the plan backfired.

Did this young woman really think I was going to spend the whole night and morning going from emergency room to emergency room, chasing nonsensical and probably nonexistent information?

I studied her. Yes, she really thought so.

"Okay," I relented. "Lenox Hill is next."

We hailed a cab. I sat back in the seat, trying to figure a way out of this mess.

On the battlefield that is the Lenox Hill Hospital emergency room, the opposing armies were now resting, exhausted. All was quiet, however temporarily.

The nurses and doctors and support staff were leaning against walls here and there, chatting with one another, or snoozing on benches.

The patients were stabilized along the walls on gurneys, waiting for rooms.

We had arrived at the tail end of a multicar accident on the FDR Drive.

No one looked at us. Everyone was dazed.

We marched up to the intake desk.

The night nurse listened to my spiel. Then she punched in the name—Abraham Lescalles—on the computer.

"He was eighty-sixed," she said. "About fourteen months ago."

I was astonished at the nurse's use of a slang term that usually signified the ejection and banishment of a patron from a bar.

"What does it mean, eighty-sixed?"

"Removal by security."

"I can't believe that," I said.

For the first time the nurse became animated. "I don't give a damn what you believe."

"Look, all—"

She put her fingers to her lips, signifying that I should lower my voice. I did.

Then she said, "Why don't you see Dr. Ahmed. He's still here. He's the one who eighty-sixed him, according to the records."

"Where is he?"

"In the lounge. Down the hall there."

Dr. Ahmed was seated at a folding table, staring into a paper cup. I could see a tea bag tag hanging sadly over the lip.

I sat down on one side of him. Emma took a chair on the other.

Ahmed, who was young and dark with large, liquid eyes, asked Emma sleepily, "Are you the angel of death?"

She smiled, showing those blinding teeth, and crossed her long legs.

"What a way to go!" Dr. Ahmed said.

I gave him my story. Then I asked. "Do you remember the man?"

"I should, shouldn't I? He punched me in the face."

"Why? For what reason?"

"That, I don't remember. But we did throw him out. Nothing unusual. We get a lot of crazies here."

"Abraham Lescalles is not a crazy."

"So you say."

"What was his complaint?"

Ahmed dunked the tea bag a couple of times, all the while focusing on Emma's legs. "Who did you say you were?" he asked.

"She's with me," I said angrily. "Please, Dr. Ahmed. We need your help."

"Okay. Okay. Let me think. Let me try to remember. What did he look like?"

I described Abraham Lescalles to the best of my ability.

Dr. Ahmed closed his eyes as if going into a trance. We waited.

"Yes," he said at last. "Right—I remember that stupid bastard."

I winced, never having heard Abraham referred to in such a manner.

"What happened?"

He opened his eyes. "A well-dressed middle-aged

man hobbled in. He refused to fill out anything or answer any nurses' questions."

"So you examined him?"

"Not really. I went into the cubicle and asked him
what the problem was. He pulled up one trouser leg
and displayed a very swollen leg. He told me that it
was phlebitis."

"Did you concur?"

"He refused to let me examine him. To even touch
him. He demanded painkillers and antibiotics."

"What happened then?"

"I said I'd have to examine him before prescribing
anything. And I told him if he really had phlebitis,
then he needed a blood thinner, not an antibiotic."

He went back to his tea bag.

"And then?"

"He slugged me."

I looked at Emma, who was tsk-tsking and wincing
in sympathy with the young doctor.

"Well, thank you," I said hurriedly and stood, mo-
tioning to Emma that we were leaving. I would try
the Plaza ploy again once out on the street. Even
Emma must be getting tired of this ridiculous investigation.

We walked out and headed toward Park Avenue.

"Hey!"

I turned. Dr. Ahmed was heading toward us.

"I forgot something. About your friend. After he
got the boot, I remember thinking that it wasn't
phlebitis."

"But how could you know that? You didn't examine him."

"I didn't know for sure. But the leg had a funny coloring. It seemed more like a bite."

"A bite?"

"Yes. Like he had been bitten by something—a scorpion, a snake, a rat—whatever. And there the antibiotics would have made sense."

He picked up where he had left off, devouring young Emma with his eyes.

This time, there was no question that the attraction was mutual. She was soaking it up, giving as good as she got.

And I couldn't have cared less.

I had had the sudden insight that I'd stumbled on something very important.

I didn't know what it meant. But I knew it meant something.

And I knew I had to tell Lucy. Now! I stared at my watch. It was two in the morning.

Dare I? Could I? Did I have any other option? No. I had to tell Lucy. I placed a hand on Ahmed's arm. "Could you make sure she gets a cab home?" I said to him.

"Markus!" Emma's voice made me cringe. "Where are you going?" She seemed to accuse me of betrayal.

"I can't explain now. Please! You're in capable hands, I'm sure."

And then I just walked away, heading uptown at a fast clip.

I stopped at the first bar I came upon. This one was particularly seedy, but there was a prominent pay phone.

I stood in front of it, sweating like a runner.

The jukebox or the tape deck was playing Bobby Darin's "Mack the Knife."

The coins were hard to grasp . . . hard to see. I dropped a quarter and a dime on the floor, bent down, felt a twinge in my back, stood up.

I consulted my watch again. How could I wake her at this hour? Particularly now, when she obviously loathed me. She would hang up on me again.

The thought came to me that this whole drama might be fake.

That the revelation about Abraham meant nothing.

So what if he had socked a doctor? So what if he might have been bitten by a rat? What did it mean?

But I couldn't help myself. The facts had filled me with a kind of dread. Of relevant dread. That I had to reveal and share. That I had to tell Lucy, or the walls of the temple would come tumbling down.

It was amazing how fast I forgot Emma.

I put the quarter into the slot. I dialed Lucy's number. One ring. Two rings. Three.

The receiver was lifted off the hook.

"Hello." A sleepy, dazed voice.

"Don't hang up the phone! Don't hang up the phone! Please, Lucy! Don't hang up the phone."

I spoke so loudly, so fast, and so imploringly that the men in the bar swiveled around on their stools to stare at me, as if I were mad. I also had the distinct impression that the bartender was reaching for a club or some other weapon behind the register.

But she didn't hang up the phone. My heart was

doing a little atrial fibrillation. Not much, mind you, but enough to make it interesting.

There was a long silence. Then: "Is that you, Markus?"

"Yes."

"Where are you?"

"In a bar, on Lexington."

"What time is it?"

"I don't know," I lied. "But it's late."

"Why did you wake me?"

"I have to see you, Lucy. Now. It's important. It's very important."

"Life-and-death, Markus? Is it a life-and-death issue?"

"Oh, yes, Lucy. Would I call you otherwise? At this hour? When I know you are through with me?"

Again there was the silence.

Then she said, "Come over."

And the phone clicked off. I hung up the receiver on my end.

I walked to the bar. The bartender approached me with narrowed eyes, smoothing his bar rag like it was my neck.

"Can I help you, boss?" he asked.

"I need something strong," I said.

"Nothing is as strong as Johnny Walker."

"Lucy Wayles is stronger."

"Never heard of it."

"Give me Wild Turkey—straight."

With a flourish that was truly aesthetic, he plucked a shot glass from the shelf and slammed it down in front of me. For some reason it seemed he had slapped something down that was lethal. Like a bullet.

I studied the small glass. A perfectly formed object. But the glass was too dense to see through to the other side.

The bartender presented the bottle for a brief second, as if it were a bottle of wine. Obviously, he was making fun of me. But who cared?

I realized that I had never tasted Wild Turkey in my life. Never. But the bird on the label was quite handsome. Lucy predicts that one day in the near future there will be flocks of wild turkeys in Central Park.

He poured the shot. Right up to the brim. Even a tiny bit over.

"Four bucks," he said.

"Keep the change," I said, handing him five.

Now it was time to drink. I studied the glass. And then leaned over the bar, without touching it with my hands, and just sipped the overdraft.

It burned my throat. My eyes began to water. My nose felt strange.

I picked up the shot glass and bolted the contents. It doubled me over. It went down to my stomach, then to my brain, then back down to my toes.

Yes, I was ready.

I walked slowly out of the bar and headed uptown on Lexington.

At Eighty-sixth Street I turned west, and then north on Madison. I was still walking slowly, an almost stately tread.

Suddenly, between Ninety-first Street and Ninety-second, a man stepped out of the doorway of a toy store.

He blocked my way.

I threw up my hands, involuntarily. But he did me no harm. He just stood there.

Was this the man who Emma thought was following us?

Then his demeanor metamorphosed.

He spat on my shoes.

I looked at him closely. His face was caked with dirt. His bedraggled suit jacket had a dead flower in one lapel. He was very tall and seemed to get taller and taller.

"Are you one of them?" I asked.

He spat again.

"Are you one of the crazy homeless people who murdered Abraham?"

I gave him some bills, stuffing them into his filthy palms, and ran around him while he was engaged in counting the loot.

He yelled after me: "It was Abraham who sacrificed Isaac!"

I was shaken. I had to compose myself. I was unraveling. It was past my bedtime.

When I reached Lucy's place, I composed myself and my attire as best I could.

I rang her bell. She buzzed me in.

I saw her standing in the doorway. I could tell by the way she stood that our conversation was going to take place in the hall.

Who cared! Just to be able to see her again. She was so lovely, standing there in her print bathrobe.

Her silvery hair took my breath away. I wanted to fall down in front of her and wrap my arms around her legs.

"I've missed you so much," I moaned.

"Get to the point, Markus. It's quite late. Have you been drinking?"

"No. Just one, Lucy. For strength."

I could not take my eyes from her. I could not fathom the extent of my loss. I would gladly have died right there, basking in her presence.

"The point, Markus. The point."

"I just came from Lenox Hill Hospital. Emergency room."

"Are you ill?"

"No. I discovered that Abraham Lescalles had gone there about fourteen months ago."

"How'd you find that out?"

"I inquired."

"But I thought we had agreed that we would no longer investigate his murder."

I was silent. I didn't want to tell her that the whole thing had been just a way to get close to Emma Pip. I didn't want to tell her that the whole thing was just a ridiculous scheme that miraculously bore fruit.

"Well, I just was so lonely without you, I had to do something or go crazy."

"Frankly, you do look crazy, Markus."

"Not as crazy as Abraham."

"What do you mean?"

"Well, he walked into Lenox Hill emergency with a swollen, painful leg. He demanded painkillers and antibiotics. The physician on duty said it looked like phlebitis and suggested a blood thinner. But Abraham wouldn't allow an examination. And he punched the doctor and got thrown out."

"So?"

"Wait. It gets better. I found the physician in question. He said that after Abraham left, he realized it probably wasn't phlebitis but some kind of bite. Maybe from a scorpion or a rat or a snake."

"So?"

"Isn't it strange?"

"Strange? Why so, Markus?"

"Because . . . well . . . because it shows an erratic streak in Abraham."

"I was bitten by two yellow jackets last year."

"Yes, I remember."

"And before that, by hornets."

"But people like Abraham don't get bitten by scorpions or snakes or whatever," I just blurted out.

Lucy, bless her, sighed, and stared at me from the doorway with a mixture of pity and concern.

"Markus, do you remember what Herodotus wrote?"

"Not off hand, Lucy."

"The Egyptians, he said, were the first to teach that the human soul is immortal, and that at the death of the body it enters into some other living thing then coming to birth—"

"But, Lucy!" I interrupted.

She held her hand up for silence and continued.

"And this soul, after passing through all creatures of land, sea, and air, enters once more into a human body at birth."

I looked down. She was barefoot like a wild Tennessee child. I realized that I would rather be in a hall-way at two-thirty in the morning being lectured on reincarnation by Lucy Wayles than in a suite at the Plaza with Emma Pip. But hadn't I always known that?

"There is a lesson to be learned here, Markus."

"What, Lucy?"

"Beware the boreal owl."

"I thought you told me to beware the tufted duck."

"No. I didn't tell you that. Your memory is faulty. But I am telling you and *only you* to beware the boreal owl."

"I'll do what you say, Lucy." Of course I hadn't the slightest idea what she was talking about.

"Good. In your condition you need a friend."

Suddenly I realized that she believed, really believed, that I was in the midst of some kind of breakdown. Suddenly I realized that she believed my hard-won information about Abraham Lescalles to be worthless, or, even worse, ridiculous.

Suddenly I felt I would shrivel up and die right there if she didn't let me hold her.

I took a step toward the door. She stopped me with a single piercing look.

"Beware the boreal owl, Markus. Remember that it has a ventriloquial ability. It can throw its melodic hoots to confuse predators and prey alike."

"Yes, dear."

"Go on home now, Markus. You need a good night's sleep. You really do."

"Yes, Lucy."

I turned as if in a daze and walked out. She was right. Fatigue was washing all over me.

I caught a cab on Fifth. Everything was going to be all right. I looked at my watch. Two forty-eight in the morning.

Everything, in fact, *was* all right. Until six in the morning.

Chapter 12

I had fallen into such a deep sleep that all I heard were little pinpricks of sound, almost like colors.

Gradually I began to realize that someone was knocking on the door.

I rolled over and hugged my pillow. Yes, someone was at the door.

In my stupor, various possibilities occurred to me. It could be Lucy apologizing for throwing me over and for not taking my Lenox Hill research seriously.

It could be Emma Pip, ready to throw herself into the bed of an aging adventurer.

It could also, I realized, be the man who delivers the *Times* in the morning, from door to door, to whom I owe nineteen dollars, which I refuse to pay because I never wanted the service. I was hoodwinked into it.

My, the knocker was persistent. I sat up. I would have to answer the door, I realized.

The clock read 6:08 A.M.

That meant I had been in a deep REM sleep for about three hours.

Enough for a soldier!

I hopped, or rather crawled, out of bed and toward the door.

The knocking kept on.

"Yes! Yes! I"m coming!"

Then, just as I reached the door, it stopped.

When I opened the door, there was no one.

My *Times* was on the mat. I peered into the hallway. All the other papers had also been delivered. I picked up my paper, noticing the pink past-due bill in the Metro section.

Who had been knocking?

I suddenly felt very light-headed. Perhaps it had been the Ghost of Christmas Past. Or the wandering soul of my uncle Harry trying to transfer to the body of a boreal owl and getting lost in traffic on the way to the transference.

I laughed. It wasn't December, and if Uncle Harry were to be reincarnated it would be as a turkey vulture.

I headed back inside.

Wait! Something else!

A package was resting against the wall next to my door.

It had a lovely wrapping—a light blue—with dark brown ribbon.

Was it for me? It was left at my door.

I took the paper and package inside and closed the door behind me.

For the first time since I rose, I realized I was butt-naked. Imagine me being out in the hallway like that. A three-hour REM nap makes one reckless.

I placed the gaily wrapped package on the bed.

Perhaps it was from Emma. Perhaps she was thanking me for the evening. Perhaps it was from Lucy, apologizing for her treatment of me. Perhaps it was something I had ordered and forgotten about. Perhaps it had been lying in that hallway for days and I just hadn't noticed it. Sometimes, as many of the Olmsted's Irregulars had pointed out, I was just plain unobservant.

I pulled the ribbon.

It wasn't a bomb.

I opened the wrapping paper.

It was worse than a bomb! It was another slab of that damn raw liver! Just like the ones that had been thrown through Lucy's window.

The wrapping was different. And something else was different.

Nestled in the horrid folds of the raw meat was an object.

I plucked it out. It was a child's rattle—the kind you find in Woolworth's for seventy-nine cents.

At first I felt fear. I was being warned. I was being threatened.

Then elation overwhelmed my fear. I had been right. Lucy had been wrong. If what I had learned about Abraham Lescalles wasn't important, why the liver?

I dressed so quickly I put on two different kinds of socks.

Then I rewrapped the liver and headed toward Central Park to confront the Lord High Executioner of the Olmsted's Irregulars.

I couldn't get a cab, even at 6:50 A.M., because a

slow drizzle was falling. And as everyone knows, when the first raindrop hits the pavement in New York, taxis head for the hills.

So I walked, ran, trotted, and crawled to the Ninetieth Street rendezvous.

They were there, all of them, in a circle, huddling against the rain.

Peter Marin saw me first. "Welcome home!" he said, beaming.

"You forgot your binoculars," Beatrice Plumb said.

"Actually, I didn't miss you at all," said John Wu.

"Oh, Markus," was all the beautiful Emma Pip could say.

Lucy Wayles said nothing. She just looked at me. Her headband was already soggy and I could see that she had not laced her birder boots all the way up.

"Here! Take a look, Lucy!"

I thrust the package out and unwrapped it.

She stared at the raw liver and the rattle.

"You see? You see?" I asked triumphantly.

The others leaned over to look.

"Isn't it a bit much for lunch?" John Wu inquired.

"Maybe he intends to make liver tartar," Beatrice noted.

Lucy took the package from me, rewrapped it, and shoved it into her knapsack.

The rain was falling harder.

"Where to?" John asked Lucy. It was a logical question. I was being ignored. Or accepted back into the group. And the main problem was the rain. Birders never abort missions during inclement weather;

they merely hole up somewhere until the weather clears.

But I had shown up for a purpose. I strode right up to Lucy and whispered in her ear, urgently, "Do you understand what I'm talking about?"

She brushed me off like I was a flea.

"We'll go to the boathouse," she said to the others.

There was a nervous silence.

The boathouse was where we all used to meet. But that was before the split, before the formation of the Olmsted's Irregulars.

The boathouse was now the territory of our rivals—the Central Park Bird-watchers.

"Is this wise?" Beatrice asked.

"Is it necessary?" John Wu asked.

"Is it dry?" Peter Marin asked, and then broke into raucous laughter at his own witticism. A second later he slipped one hand surreptitiously around Emma's shoulder. She shook it off neatly.

"Let's go," Lucy said.

And they trudged off. I stood my ground. Was I still a member of the group? I didn't know. Should I even try? After all, its leader had abandoned me and made fun of me.

"Oh, come on!" Lucy called back to me impatiently.

I fell into the line of march, hanging my head like the feeble child I felt myself to be, carrying nothing but my psychic bruises.

The boathouse in Central Park is a jewel. It sits on the northeast edge of the lake, between East Drive and the Ramble.

It contains tables, food concessions, a café, rowboats for rental, and an outdoor porch right on the lake.

And above all, it contains "the Book," chained to a table.

This is a large loose-leaf book in which bird-watchers record their sightings for others to peruse.

One can walk into the boathouse and just open the Book. And see what birds are about, and where. It is more than just a list. It contains reflections, directions, jokes, and philosophical aphorisms pertaining to birds.

And, before the split, Lucy had even introduced drawings.

The Book had even been used to catch a criminal. And a very nefarious one at that.

It had been late last summer. Deep in the Ramble, one of the birders had stumbled on a horrible sight. A small, thin stick was stuck in the ground among the exposed root system of a sycamore tree. The stick was coated with a strong glue. One bird had already been caught on it.

More glued sticks were found and it was obvious there was a dangerous poacher in the park catching birds either to eat, to sell, or just out of cruelty.

The Book became the central information source on this individual until he was caught . . . and caught he was.

As we all entered the boathouse that rainy morning, one could feel the tension.

It could turn out like a meeting between the Earps and the Clancy brothers. It could be another shoot-out at the O.K. Corral.

They were there! At least six birders from the Central Park Bird-watchers, including Paula Fox and Jack Mowbray.

They were lounging across two tables, their binoculars still in the cases, gazing sadly out over the lake.

We filed silently by and occupied two other tables. Only a single unoccupied table separated us.

Then Lucy began to act very strangely. She stood up and waved her arms. Everyone in the two groups stared at her.

"Good news! Good news! It's Markus's birthday, and the coffee's on him."

Everybody applauded. Lucy nudged me. "Get the coffee, Markus."

I whispered in her ear, "But it's not my birthday, Lucy."

"Get the coffee!"

I walked to the counter and ordered. I heard a few yells behind me. "I want tea! I want hot chocolate!"

When the orders were finally sorted out, I carried the containers back and distributed them to the two birder groups.

But Lucy wasn't finished.

Gleefully she shouted out: "And he brought something to have with the coffee."

Then, to my horror, she reached into her knapsack, extricated the package, and exposed the raw liver for all to see.

"Is this a birthday cake, or what?" she asked, laughing.

There were groans and jeers and cynical applause.

Then she picked up the child's rattle and shook it.

"And he brought a party favor," she said to the assembled.

More laughter. More applause.

She picked up one bloody piece of liver and held it high.

"Who wants the first slice?"

There were groans of disgust.

But then one voice—it was Paula Fox's—called out: "Give it to Willy Five."

There were shouts of approval. All kinds of shouts. "Willy Five. Give it to Willy."

Now, I knew who Willy Five was. A feral cat who lived under the huge rock that abutted the boathouse on the side of the Ramble.

He was named after the original Willy—a legendary Central Park cat.

I never knew him. But Lucy did. His antics were often remarkable, if the stories are true. One time, it is said, the mayor attended a ground-breaking ceremony for a playground in the park. A bulldozer was used for breaking the ground. When the shovel filled with dirt, it was elevated preparatory to dumping the dirt into a waiting truck.

Then a loud wail came from on high. Lo and behold, Willy was in the shovel, on top of the dirt, screeching out his anger.

Another time, a horse and buggy passed under the famous crouching black panther statue on the East Drive around Seventy-seventh Street.

The driver pointed the statue out to his passengers—two retired teachers from Canada.

A second later the statue seemed to come to life.

The panther had leaped into the cab. The horse reared. The driver fell off. The passengers went into shock.

Of course, it was only Willy.

"Willy Five it is," Lucy agreed. "Come along, Markus."

We left to prolonged applause.

Lucy was moving so fast I had trouble keeping up with her.

We climbed the rock and Lucy flung the liver down a cranny.

"Why did you embarrass me like that?" I gasped out. "This was between you and me. This was about us."

"Markus, you are becoming an old fuddy-duddy."

I didn't get a chance to respond. She put one hand to her lips and pointed with the other.

A low-slung, thuggish-looking cat was crawling through the drizzled terrain. He climbed the rock, keeping one eye on us and one on the liver. It was obvious he didn't like bird-watchers.

"That's him. That's Willy Five," she whispered. "See the all-black coat with the white ruff? The same as Willy One. But look at the legs. Not Willy One at all. White splotch on left front and right rear. More like Willies Three and Four."

"What happened to the other Willies?" I asked.

"Some gone, I guess. Some alive and well in other parts of the park. Willy One was a lothario. He left all kinds of Willies."

The cat pulled a piece of liver loose and ran off with it.

We stood there until he had vanished from sight. The rain was letting up. The sun seemed to be struggling to come out.

Suddenly, Lucy took my hand and held it tightly.

I became so excited . . . so overcome with affection for her . . . so happy to feel her friendship again that I couldn't say a damn word, even though I tried.

She turned, looked me in the eye, and kissed me lightly on the mouth.

A thousand guitars. A trip to the moon.

"Oh, Lucy, does this mean you forgive me? Does this mean you'll see me again? Does this mean we are together again?"

She smiled and cocked her head.

"Was it ever otherwise, Markus?"

My God! Had the woman gone mad?

"Lucy!" I yelled. "Yes. It was otherwise. You told me you didn't want to see me anymore. You wouldn't even answer my calls. You made me miserable for days! You said you had met someone else."

"Someone else?" she asked innocently.

"Yes. A man named Duke."

"This may all be a misunderstanding," Lucy said.

"No misunderstanding! You ended our relationship abruptly. You implied that you loved Duke."

Lucy smiled again. She looked at the sky.

"It's clearing, Markus."

I shook my head. I didn't want to talk about the weather.

"Markus, did I ever tell you the story about Willy One and the horse and buggy?"

"Yes."

"Did you ever hear about Willy Three and the mugger?"

"No. And I don't want to hear it. Stop changing the subject, Lucy! I want to deal with reality."

"Reality, Markus? Is that right?"

"Yes!"

"Well, if you really want to deal with reality, it's time you met Duke."

"I don't want to meet your new lover. I want you to leave him. I want you to come back to me. Isn't that why you held my hand like that just now? Isn't that why you kissed me?"

She replied, "This afternoon, Markus, at four-thirty. Be on the corner of Fifty-eighth and First."

She walked away.

"I won't share you, Lucy! No matter my misery, it's all or nothing at all."

She walked back into the boathouse.

I couldn't go back in there. I couldn't stay where I was.

So I walked out of the park and took a cab home to get some more sleep.

Chapter 13

I got up at two in the afternoon. I felt good. I felt strong. I looked out the window. The rain had stopped.

Lucy wanted me to be at Fifty-eighth and First at four-thirty. There was plenty of time to shower and dress.

I flirted, very briefly, with not going. What Lucy wants, Lucy gets. If she wants me to meet Duke, I will. After all, Lucy and I were almost back together. She had held my hand, kissed me, even claimed that she had never dumped me. That was progress.

But all kinds of ideas were now percolating in my head.

It seemed possible to me now that all the time she had been seeing me, she had had lovers on the side.

There may have been several Dukes . . . a whole slew of Dukes. And all the while I had in my head that Lucy was just a little bit prim.

I wondered who the newest Duke was . . . the one I was meeting.

I wondered what he looked like. Oh, I knew I'd be

meeting him in an hour or two, but I couldn't help speculating.

He probably was one of those tall, thin, blond, acerbic investment bankers. He probably looked forty, even though he was seventy, and liked to sail. Duke was probably just a childhood nickname. His real name had to be Roger or Timothy.

No, I realized, that wasn't Lucy's taste.

He will probably turn out to be a short, thin, very handsome South American painter . . . whose real name was Jorge.

No, I thought, that was ridiculous. He will probably be a rugged, craggy Australian bird-watcher who could live off the land in the outback like an aborigine.

It was best, I thought, to dress simply. After all, maybe Lucy was setting up a duel. For her hand. An Arthurian joust.

Who knew with Lucy?

Maybe she was at the stage of her life when she wanted suitors to fight over her.

The problem was, I was kind of old and weak and out of shape.

Anyway, I dressed "sporting." Including a rather rakish hat.

I left the apartment at three forty-five and walked slowly to Fifty-eighth Street and First Avenue, arriving at twenty past four.

What a mess I found. Three out of the four corners, including two lanes of First Avenue, were being ripped up by the gas and telephone companies. Smoke and steam were billowing upward toward the under-belly of the Fifty-ninth Street Bridge.

What a ridiculous spot for Lucy to have selected.

Only one space was safe—on the southwest corner, between a Mexican restaurant and two public phones.

So there is where I waited, like an innocent near the fires of hell.

I had no idea why they were digging up the street, but it was a fearsome spectacle. From time to time I could swear that I saw real flames interspersed among the billowing steam jets.

Because of the digging, First Avenue was backed up for blocks, and it seemed that all the irate motorists were honking their horns at one time. Like a flock of geese, as Lucy would note, whose leader had taken the wrong direction.

At four-thirty, Lucy hadn't shown.

To make matters worse, it started to drizzle again.

To make matters much worse, the stupid public phone began to ring.

Soon, the horns and the steam, the phone and all the street noise started bouncing around in my head.

Still, Lucy did not show.

I couldn't stand much more of the general situation, and no more of that jangling phone. I walked to the phone booth, picked up the phone, and yelled, "There's no one here! There's no one here!"

I was about to hang up when I heard, to my absolute astonishment, the measured voice of Lucy Wayles.

"Is that you, Markus?"

"Is that you, Lucy?"

"Of course."

"What is going on? Where are you? Why are you calling a public phone?"

"To speak to you, silly. So you're on time."

"I'm always on time. But you're not."

"I'm running just a tick late, Markus. Why don't you walk to Fifty-ninth. I'll be coming east down Fifty-ninth."

"When?"

"Now."

"I'm very confused, Lucy."

"You always say that. Good-bye, Markus."

She hung up. I walked the one block to Fifty-ninth and stared west, toward Second Avenue.

I did not see Lucy. I waited. I peered through the drizzle.

Then, suddenly, the sun burst through again and I could see a familiar figure walking toward me. But she was alone. Where was Duke?

She came closer. Now I could see that, indeed, she was not alone.

She had a dog on a leash!

The dog seemed to be pulling her in between staggers. Was the dog drunk?

She was very close now. I removed my hat—startled by what I saw next.

The dog she was walking had only three legs!

And worse, it was a pit bull!

A young, powerfully built brindle, three-legged pit bull terrier.

Lucy stopped right in front of me. She pointed to my hat. "Nice hat," she said. "You rarely wear one."

Then she asked, "He's compensating quite well, Markus . . . isn't he?"

She didn't wait for my answer. She bent over and addressed the dog: "Duke. This is Markus."

Then she addressed me: "Markus. This is Duke."

I was bewildered. "*The* Duke? *Your* Duke?"

Lucy laughed. "He most definitely is *the* Duke. But he's not *my* Duke. He lives at the Humane Society, down the block. And I'm just one of his volunteer walkers. His real owner is dead, Markus. From what I hear, a very bad man. A drug dealer. There was a shoot-out in Queens. The DEA and Duke's gang. Poor Duke got caught in the cross fire."

I didn't know what to say. Duke kept staring at me. He made me very nervous.

"They're dangerous dogs, Lucy," was all I could finally contribute.

"Nonsense. Duke's a pussycat. And a brave one at that."

She held out her arm. I took it. The three of us hopped together back to Duke's motel.

After three-legged Duke had been safely delivered back to his cell and we were out on the street again, Lucy said, "I'm famished, Markus. Let's eat."

"Isn't it a little early for you?"

"Yes. But who knows what the night will bring? We need strength, dear."

I must confess, I felt a tremor of erotic anticipation. Was that what she meant? An assignation in my apartment? Oh, Lucy! Would it be so! Would I be equal to it?

And then I felt an equally powerful perplexity.

Only a few days ago she wanted absolutely nothing to do with me. Now she was hinting at intimacy, even ecstasy.

"Let's walk west on Fifty-seventh Street, Markus. We can window-shop as we look for a restaurant."

"Yes," I agreed happily. That would mean we were walking toward my apartment.

So, off we went, arm in arm.

At Third Avenue, Lucy asked, "Did I ever tell you about my childhood, Markus?"

"I think you might have."

"It was a happy childhood. We were poor but happy. Very poor."

"So I understand."

"But in the eighteenth century, the Wayleses were in Tidewater, Virginia, not Hardscrabble, Tennessee, where I grew up. We had land, Markus, and slaves, and grand houses and harpsichords and dancing teachers and books with beautiful bindings. Did you know that?"

"I believe you told me. The slaves must have been quite happy with your harpsichord."

We passed many restaurants. But none of them seemed to suit her fancy this evening.

When we reached Eighth Avenue, she inexplicably turned left—downtown.

A block and a half later she stopped, pointed, and announced, "We'll eat here."

I found myself staring at the Donegal Star, a very disreputable drinking spot with an equally disreputable hot-plate counter. It masqueraded as a working-class Irish pub.

"You can't be serious," I protested.

"I'm quite serious. We need stick-to-the-ribs food."

She marched in. Like Queen Guinevere inspecting the stables. I followed.

The bar was crowded with a rakish assortment of Eighth Avenue denizens.

There was no line at the hot-plate counter.

"You get the food and I'll get the drinks, Markus, and we'll meet in a booth in the back."

How romantic, I thought.

Then she gave me her order.

"I want a hot brisket plate, mashed potatoes with gravy, and green beans."

That was definitely not Lucy's usual fare.

"Lucy, the brisket is full of fat. The gravy is pure grease. And the beans are canned."

"All the better," she said, and headed for the bar.

I filled her order and took a piece of roast chicken for myself. Then I loaded the tray and headed for a back booth.

Lucy was waiting for me, as she often waited, sitting very erect and seemingly lost in thought.

"What is this?" I asked, pointing at the four full steins she had arranged soldierlike in the center of the booth.

"Ale, Markus. For strength."

I distributed the food. Lucy ate with gusto and curiosity, studying each piece of food as if it were a totally alien cuisine.

My chicken tasted like old London broil.

Halfway through, she suddenly pushed the dish

away, took a long drink of ale, smacked her lips, and said, "Markus, I have reached a conclusion."

"About what?"

"About life. It is time for us to put away childish things."

"By all means."

"Yes, Markus. It is time for us to get back to basics. To forget about poor Abraham Lescalles. To forget about those ridiculous stolen watercolors. To forget about everything that is not essential."

"I agree."

"Just you and I, Markus. And the creatures of the air. And Olmsted's Irregulars."

I felt a warm glow. Yes, we were truly back together. I took a very long drink of the ale. Three steins had now been consumed.

"Yes. We must now put away childish things, Markus," she repeated. She grabbed my hand. "The birds, Markus. Study the birds."

"Yes Lucy." She was getting drunk?

"And, Markus, we must always remember to do justice, love mercy, and walk humbly with our God."

"Of course, Lucy."

She sighed, let go of my hand, and sat back in the booth.

We shared the last ale. The other booths were now full. The noise level was rising. Burly men shunted back and forth between booth and bar, reeking of sweat, carrying pitchers of beer and shots of whiskey.

It was so odd of Lucy to have wanted to come in here, so unlike her.

"Do you know what I would like to do now?"

Again, my heart skipped a beat at the question. My apartment was only a few blocks away.

"What?"

"Take a stroll."

I groaned.

"But, Lucy. It's not even seven o'clock. You usually take your strolls around midnight."

"Indulge me, Markus. That's what I crave. A slow stroll. Maybe up Fifth Avenue along the park. Wouldn't you like that?"

We left the bar five minutes later. The rain had stopped but it was foggy. And a chilly wind was blowing up.

We walked east on Fifty-seventh Street and then north on Fifth Avenue.

At Sixty-second Street she asked, "Do you miss working?"

"Very rarely."

"Oh, I miss it all the time. I so loved the Archives. I so loved being a librarian."

"Yes, it must have been exciting," I noted wryly.

"It was! It really was. Like being a matchmaker. Like making beautiful weddings."

"You've lost me there, Lucy."

"Ah, you don't understand. We bring together the writers and the readers . . . the poets and the people who crave a new language . . . the artists and those who search for beauty . . . the entomologists and those fascinated with bugs . . . the psychiatrists and those who want to peer into their own heads. Matchmaking! Every day, Markus, the items used to cross my desk. Books, pamphlets, journals, slides, portfolios, tapes, movies. And I catalogued them and processed them because someone out there, one day, would want them."

She stopped. She stared at me.

"Do you understand?"

My, she was getting worked up over nothing.

"Yes, Lucy."

"Remember, Markus, the librarian of the great library in ancient Alexandria was considered the first citizen of the city."

"Wasn't that the library that went up in flames?"

"Yes. The Roman fleet torched it. One of the great tragedies of humankind. More than a million papyrus rolls were destroyed, containing knowledge that has never been recovered."

"They could have used a smoke alarm."

My quip went flat. We walked on.

The fog was thicker. It was cooler. The darkness was coming early.

At Seventieth Street Lucy stopped dead in her tracks.

"What's the matter?"

"Listen!"

"To what?"

"Just listen!" She cocked her head to one side.

"I hear nothing."

"Music."

I strained but I could not hear anything but street noise.

"It's getting louder. Do you hear it now?"

"No."

"A harpsichord, Markus."

I turned around slowly in place, my ears straining.

"No, Lucy. I do not hear a note . . . not a single one."

"It's not real, Markus. I am talking about the birds."

"I hear no birds."

"Not birdsong. Listen. Don't you hear their rustling . . . the sounds of dusk? The rustling of their wings as they prepare for night."

"I hear no rustling."

"Sure you do, Markus. Work at it. You'll hear them all—the thrushes and warblers and tanagers and cardinals—the sparrows and kestrels and woodcocks—the owls and the buntings. It's like the Goldberg Variations."

She took my hand and squeezed it. I truly believed that what Lucy Wayles needed at that moment was a strong sedative.

"Shouldn't I take you home?" I asked.

"But it's a lovely stroll."

And we kept walking uptown.

The moment we crossed the Seventy-second Street Transverse, Lucy made a sharp left turn.

"Wait!" I said, pulling her to a stop.

"Why?"

"We can't go into the park now."

"Why?"

"It's almost dark, Lucy. It's dangerous."

"Nonsense, Markus. I want to hear the music."

"How far in are we going?"

"Not far. Nothing to worry about."

We strolled in, going slowly due west along the road. The benches, where by day hundreds of New

Yorkers stopped to rest or eat their lunches or neck with their beloveds, were now empty.

Even the joggers seemed to have abandoned the fog and drizzle and darkness.

"Lucy, this is not a good idea," I said, trying to slow her down and turn her around.

"It's a wonderful idea, Markus. I feel like dancing."

Then she moved away from me and actually broke into a sort of Highland fling that took her to the edge of the steep steps going down to Bethesda Fountain.

"I am not going down there," I announced.

"Nor am I," she said gaily, taking my arm again and guiding me deeper into the park.

We reached the southwest edge of the lake and headed north along the West Drive path.

The people seemed to have vanished. All I could see were the headlights of cars on my left.

To my right were the woods that ringed the lake shore.

I cringed. The arms of hidden assassins seemed to keep reaching out from the trees. My back was wet from the exertion of repressing panic.

Suddenly, Lucy stooped and whispered in my ear, almost playfully, "You'll never guess what I am going to tell you, Markus."

I was silent and grim.

"I have to go to the bathroom."

"Then let's get out of here and go into a bar or restaurant," I said, thankful for a reason to escape the park.

"I mean now, Markus. Right now!"

"But there's no place—"

"By the lake," she interrupted.

"Lucy, you can't go through those woods now."

"It'll take only a minute, Markus."

She headed off the path.

"Wait! Please! Don't go in there, Lucy!"

"Stop being such a baby, Markus. It's as safe as my bathroom at home."

"I'm begging you, Lucy."

"My Lord, you *are* silly. Look, why don't you just wait a minute or two and then follow after me. We'll keep in touch by shouting to each other."

I was about to protest more when she held out her finger in an accusing gesture.

"Stop this nonsense, Markus. You're such an alarmist. I'll make it even safer. If one of us gets lost, we'll just meet somewhere that both of us knows well."

"Where?"

"How about the Eaglevale Bridge?"

"Is that where Abraham was murdered?"

"No! And it's not the bridge we always eat lunch under, either. Wake up, Markus! It's that small stone arch over the bridle path that leads onto West Seventy-seventh Street. The one with the statue of Humboldt."

Then she vanished from sight. I remembered that I once knew who Humboldt was.

How long did she say I should wait before coming after her?

I started counting: One one thousand; two one thousand; three one thousand.

Wait! Something was peculiar, I realized. Why was

she going all the way down to the lake if she had to "go" so badly?

Why not just in the woods?

Girl Scouts go in the woods. they're not afraid of bugs and such.

I stepped off the path and into the brush.

"Lucy!" I called out.

She answered me. I felt better.

I made my way another ten feet.

It was like an overgrown Indian trail. There were vines and creepers coming from above.

"Lucy!" I called out again.

She answered me, but from farther away and slightly north.

I stumbled over a cache of empty beer bottles. Rolling Rock.

The air had turned damp and fetid and it seemed to be smothering me.

"Lucy!" I called out again.

This time there was no answer.

It occurred to me that she had done what she had to do and was working her way back to me. There was no reason to call out again. I waited.

But she didn't appear.

"Lucy! Lucy!" I started to call out every five seconds.

No response!

I started to move quickly toward the lake.

"Lucy! Lucy! Lucy!"

No response. No sound.

I moved faster. I tried to run. I fell down. I got up.

And then I realized that I didn't really know where the hell the lake was.

I couldn't see it. I didn't know which way I was facing.

I started taking three steps this way and three steps that way, like a drunken chicken.

My eyes strained for a break in the trees that would signal shoreline—but I saw nothing.

I squatted on the ground, frightened, exhausted, ashamed. I was lost in Central Park. Who would believe it?

I waited there for I know not what. I found myself listening to what seemed to be a low hum.

I was so confused by then that it must have taken me a full five minutes to realize that the hum was cars.

And another five minutes to realize that cars meant the road—the West Drive.

I ran out of the woods, honing in on the hum, my trousers damp and soiled.

Lucy was not on the drive. But I remembered what she had told me . . . that if either of us got lost we would meet at the West Seventy-seventh Street bridge.

I looked around to get my bearings, using the Central Park West buildings outside the park as my referents.

The bridge should be just across the drive and only a few blocks north.

I covered the distance in record time for frightened, overweight males.

But no one was there to reward me. Lucy was not there. Not yet.

Was she still wandering, lost, on the lake shore? Didn't she know the landmarks? Of course she did.

What if something horrible really had happened?

But there had been no screams.

A vision of Lucy being hit over the head and crumbling silently to earth made me tremble.

I stood on the deserted stone bridge and stared out in all directions, like Ahab on the *Pequod*.

A police car cruised by just outside the park, and I stepped back into the shadows. I was worried about the dangerous criminals lurking all over the park. But what if the police took me for one of the very people I feared? They might blast me into the next world, writing me off as just another drug dealer or pervert.

I started a little singsong to keep my spirits up.

Yes . . . I was gradually losing my mind. I felt myself being drawn back to the woods near the lake . . . where I would crash through the brush yelling out her name . . . run along the lake shore until I found Lucy's poor battered body.

What a nightmare this stroll had become.

I saw the police car again.

When do I flag them down and tell them that my love has gone . . . that poor Lucy never returned . . . that she had been raped, murdered, and cut into small pieces by a fiend?

Then I heard a sound from beneath the bridge . . . from the riding path.

It was too late for a horse and rider. It had to be Lucy, finding her way back by the path.

I ran down the slope onto it.

All I could see, under the arch, were workmen's tools and plastic bags.

An ugly steel door was open.

Obviously the arch itself contained a storage room, and there were park maintenance workers cleaning up in there.

I started to climb back up the slope.

But them I realized that the maintenance workers could help me. They surely would know how to find missing persons in Central Park. I poked my head past the corroded steel door and into the space.

It was no time to be subtle.

"Hello! Can you help me? I need help."

I found myself face to face with three maintenance workers.

They didn't respond to me at all.

Then I realized they weren't maintenance workers.

One of them, a woman, said, "Hello, Markus."

Another one, a younger woman, said, "How nice to see you, Markus."

Astonishing. It was Beatrice Plumb and Emma Pip.

The third one, a man, didn't say a word.

He did look vaguely familiar, however.

But I truly didn't recognize him until he raised the shovel he was holding high over his head and started toward me.

It was that doorman from Abraham Lescalles's hotel: Mr. Nolan.

My whole life didn't flash before my eyes but I surely knew I was going to die.

A rogue doorman was going to smash my skull to smithereens.

I was a dead Markus.

I could see the shovel coming down but I couldn't move.

Then I heard the explosion. Right behind my ear. It deafened me. I could smell something strange.

Nolan was no longer in front of me.

He had been thrown on his back, his shovel hand oddly twisted and bleeding.

I turned and started to crawl out of that horrible place.

I bumped into a pair of legs.

The bump knocked me backwards. I looked up.

An old woman in a straw hat was standing calmly with a shotgun in her arms.

Emma Pip and Beatrice Plumb were now cowering beside the fallen doorman.

"Lookee here," the lady shotgunner said, walking over to three large wooden boxes that lined one wall of the shed.

It was the first time I had noticed them. They looked like ammunition boxes in the old U.S. Army— before they had changed from wood to aluminum.

The old lady slipped one glove on, kicked open a box, reached in with the gloved hand, and pulled out the largest rattlesnake I had ever seen.

"Lookee here," she said again. "A real black diamondback rattler. Damn!"

She held the writhing snake up and looked at me.

I cringed on the ground. I was surrounded by crazy people.

The old lady brought the snake closer to my face. She recited:

"And the signs shall follow them that believe;
In my name shall they cast out devils;
They shall speak with new tongues;
They shall take up serpents;
And if they drink any deadly thing, it shall not hurt them;
They shall lay hands on the sick, and they shall recover."

All I remember thinking was that this crazy old lady was going to let the snake sink its poison fangs into me. That was the real reason she saved me from Nolan and his shovel—so she could quote the Gospel of Mark and then kill me. It seemed rational.

"Aunt Hattie! This is no time for fun and games."

Lucy! I turned to the voice.

Yes! It was Lucy!

I turned back to the old woman.

This was her legendary aunt Hattie! Where had she come from?

"Put the snake back, Aunt Hattie," Lucy ordered.

Then Lucy stared at me.

"What are you doing on the floor, Markus? You don't look hurt."

I couldn't speak.

"Here's a quarter, Markus," she said, pressing a coin into my hand. "The minute you can get up, please find a pay phone and dial 911."

I'd heard those words before. The last time, it had also meant murder.

Chapter 14

An hour later, Aunt Hattie, Lucy, and I were seated on the now familiar bench of the Central Park precinct house.

An agitated Detective Jim Loach paced up and down about five feet away.

He kept approaching, staring, cursing, and then backing off.

"Okay, okay," he finally said. "The doorman is at Bellevue. Once his elbow gets put back together again, we'll book him for assault with a deadly weapon and attempted murder."

He pointed a finger at me. "You did say he tried to kill you with that shovel, didn't you?"

I nodded. Lucy patted me on the knee as if my nod were truly heroic.

Loach continued. "We're holding the two women on a variety of charges: trespassing; destruction of park property; possession of poisonous reptiles; and whatever else we can think of. The bomb squad took the snakes to the Bronx Zoo."

Now he pointed at Lucy.

"But you're going to tell me all about how those

three loonies murdered Abraham Lescalles. Am I correct?"

"Correct," Lucy affirmed.

"I'll take that statement in a few minutes. You people just stay put."

Then he glared at Aunt Hattie.

"And what the hell were you doing in the park with a loaded shotgun?"

"Squirrel," said Aunt Hattie pleasantly.

"What?"

"New York squirrel. Hear it's the best. Me and this ole boy next to me needed some supper."

"You were going to shoot and eat New York squirrels."

"Yep. Gotta braise 'em with orange peels, then put 'em in a skillet with carrots and onions and peanut oil and a little rye whiskey."

Loach held up his hand. He didn't want to hear any more. He gave a huge sigh, perhaps of desperation, then vanished up the stairs.

"That young man seems hard to please, Lucy," Aunt Hattie noted.

Then she leaned over and patted me on the head like I was a hunting dog.

"I like this beau of your'n, Lucy. But he's kinda long in the tooth for you."

"Is everything okay, Markus? You look poorly."

"Nothing is okay," I replied.

"But you did a yeomanlike job, Markus. You're a hero. You broke the case."

"Lucy. Isn't it time you told me what's going on?"

"Poor man! Yes, you deserve the truth, the whole truth, and nothing but the truth."

"Thank you."

"Do you want it from the beginning or from the end?"

Aunt Hattie whispered in my ear, "Take it from the end, son. She's famous for being long-winded."

"From anyplace, " I said to Lucy. My feet were beginning to fall asleep.

Lucy made a gesture that I should follow her away from the bench. I did so.

She said quietly, "Aunt Hattie seems to be upsetting you, Markus. Let me explain. We're a very genteel family. And believe me, Aunt Hattie has caused us no small embarrassment over the years. So you just have to learn to live with her. She does have her strong points."

"No doubt."

We returned to the bench.

Aunt Hattie was taking a quick nap, her straw hat bobbing up and down with every little snore.

Lucy was silent.

"Well?"

"Yes?"

"You were going to tell me why that Mr. Nolan tried to behead me."

"Of course. Let me start from the middle. That would be the easiest way to proceed because it is very complex, Markus. And there has been so much violence."

"Lucy. Why don't you just tell it to me the way you're going to tell it to Detective Loach."

The mention of the detective's name roused Aunt Hattie.

"I wouldn't say a word to that rude young man. Lucy, put some pepper on his nose! Like I did with Beezy's dog. Do you remember that dog?"

"Aunt Hattie, please. I'm busy."

Aunt Hattie winked at me, folded her arms, and stared straight ahead.

"Let me start with Sylvia Rand, Markus."

"By all means."

"The woman is living with cancer. She doesn't know yet whether or not it will kill her. But like many cancer victims she begins to search for something new in her life . . . something that will give her strength, wisdom, courage, hope. That's normal, isn't it, Markus?"

"Quite normal."

"Yes . . . well—"

Aunt Hattie interrupted again. "Always had that gift of gab. She always did."

We both ignored her now. Lucy continued.

"She begins to exercise. She goes bird-watching. She does a great many things, but nothing brings her peace. She knows she has only so long to live, but she really can't find what she needs. She really doesn't know what she wants. And then she meets a man in church."

Aunt Hattie let out another hoot. "Only thing you can tell about a man in church is whether he has a pair of shoes."

I was learning how to screen out Hattie's voice. "You mean Abraham Lescalles?"

"Yes. And Abraham tells her about a small group of people who assemble in Central Park at night in a secret place and practice a profound but very dangerous kind of faith."

"You lost me," I said.

"Picking up serpents, Markus. What do you think those rattlers were doing there? Haven't you ever heard of snake-handling churches?"

"Yes. I've heard of them."

"Well, that was what was going on. That's what Abraham Lescalles created, believe it or not: a small snake-handling church, no different from a thousand others that spring up every year in the mountains of West Virginia and Tennessee. Only this is New York."

"Where did he get the snakes?"

"On his so-called camping trips down South. They are not hard to acquire or transport, Markus."

This whole story of hers was getting more perplexing as it unraveled.

"But why do Christians want to pick up serpents, Lucy?"

"Faith. A test of faith. If your faith is strong, a rattler's poison will not kill you. If your faith is very strong, the rattler will not even strike."

I could not imagine Emma or Beatrice or Abraham even thinking about such a test.

"Let me return to Sylvia Rand," Lucy said.

"Please do."

"She has become a communicant in Abraham's church. Her world is expanding spiritually. Abraham begins to trust her. He asks her for a favor."

"A sexual favor?"

"Of course not. Don't be lewd, Markus. Abraham had learned that the small storage room he discovered under the Eaglevale Bridge was drawn by Harlow Trent early in the park's history. I don't know how he found out. But he did. And he asked Sylvia to steal that specific drawing from the Archives to protect the secrecy of the cult."

"That was stupid," I noted.

"Paranoid. No doubt. But any man who believes as he believed must have been touched by paranoia. More than touched . . . . swamped. Most likely he also instructed Sylvia to take three other drawings to obscure the reason for the theft."

"But how did you find that out, Lucy? I was with you when you went to the Historical Society to look at the slides. You didn't notice any secret door then."

"Don't call it a secret door, Markus. It's rather an obscure door. My friend Davey sent me blowups of the slides. I used a magnifying glass on them."

I burst into inappropriate laughter. It was just too much to imagine—Lucy with a big magnifying glass. Like she was Sherlock Holmes. And I must be Watson.

Lucy glared at me. "If you find murder funny, Markus, perhaps I'd better get another listener."

"No, no, Lucy. Please."

"Very well. Anyway, that's how I found the door in the arch of Eaglevale Bridge. There are probably a dozen similar hidden storage rooms that were originally built into the bridges and have now been sealed shut or forgotten. Only the sparrows know them, and they tell no one. Not even Olmsted's Irregulars."

Aunt Hattie suddenly stood up, stretched, and sat down, grumbling at something. Her hat was perched crazily on the side of her head.

"And then Sylvia Rand died," Lucy said ominously.

"Yes. I remember when Sheila Ott told us how her sister had killed herself when the cancer became too much to bear."

"I don't think she killed herself, Markus."

"What?" I was startled. "You mean she was murdered?"

"Yes and no. I mean, she was bitten by a snake during a church service. Probably in the worst spot: the neck. A doctor was out of the question. She was in her death throes. They took her farther into the park in her own car and shot her through the neck to obscure the snakebites. They typed a suicide note. Everyone knew she had terminal cancer. There would be no autopsy."

I found myself being more and more drawn into Lucy's narrative. Oh, I always liked listening to her—but she was often illogical. Or went spinning off on tangents. Not now!

"Are you sure she died that way?"

"It makes sense, Markus. Down home, picking up snakes is also used for healing. Sylvia probably started to participate with abandon. It seemed a better option than radiation or chemotherapy."

"So Sylvia was gone from the church of the rattlesnake."

"Gone forever."

"Did the church disband?"

"No!"

"Who else was in it?"

"Well, there was Emma and Nolan and Beatrice—and there had to be several others whose names we don't know yet."

"And Abraham Lescalles, the 'pillar of the community' who was leading a secret life as a fire-breathing snake preacher."

"Exactly."

"Why was it so secret?"

"Illegal, for one. And frowned upon, for another. It has even less acceptance than something like the peyote church, where people sit in the desert and swallow hallucinogens."

"And the murder, Lucy?"

"Lescalles?"

"Yes."

"I believe he was murdered by the three you found in that shed. I believe that Mr. Nolan, to get the police to drop your assault charge, will confess that all three participated; he'll characterize himself, of course, as an unwilling participant."

"But why?"

"Why?"

"Yes. Why?"

Aunt Hattie chimed in: "A good man never asks why."

We both ignored her.

"Abraham had lost his faith."

"But he was their leader."

"Yes."

"And so what if he lost his faith? Why kill him?"

"Here is what I think happened, Markus. After the

death of Sylvia, her grisly death, Abraham became very nervous over what had transpired."

"You mean the faking of the suicide."

"Yes! Remember, down South when a parishioner dies from a snakebite in a snake-handling church, the preacher is indicted as an accessory to murder. Abraham realized they had done something very wrong. The Holy Spirit was obviously not among them. His faith wavered. And then *he* was bitten. On the leg. Probably while feeding the snake."

Lucy shook her head slowly, sadly, as if she could see it happening in her mind's eye.

"And he did something that no self-respecting snake handler ever does. He sought medical help for the bite. *You* discovered that, Markus!"

"Yes, I did," I said proudly.

"I believe that his intention then was to close the church down and report to the police all the events surrounding the death of Sylvia Rand. At this point, faced with the loss of their cherished rituals and the possible loss of their freedom, they murdered him."

"What a horrible story!"

"And to make matters worse, Markus, I think each of them slashed Abraham in turn. A kind of group murder. All with the same knife. Then they hid Abraham's shoes and money to make it seem a crime committed by the homeless."

Lucy gave a huge sigh and concluded: "So that, I think, Markus, is the whole ball of wax. And I think it will all be shown to be true from the mouths of the murderers themselves. And what I told you is what I am going to tell Detective Loach."

I leaned back as far as I could, luxuriating in the end of the tale.

My goodness! Lucy had been brilliant.

It was incredible, also, how valuable my contribution had been.

Of course, I realized luck had played a disproportionately important role.

Just plain old dumb luck.

I mentioned this fact to Lucy.

"What luck, Markus?" she asked.

"Why, the luck we had at every step of the way. If you hadn't decided to dump me, for example, I wouldn't have made a laughingstock of myself with Emma Pip. And then I would never have played detective and found out about Abraham's bites. And you would never have had a clue about the secret snake-handling church in the park."

I waited for a response. She didn't answer. That was strange.

"And it was even luckier that you got lost in the park tonight, Lucy. If you hadn't gotten lost, I never would have ended up on that stone bridge. I never would have heard them in that old storage room."

Again she was silent.

"Lucy? Do you hear me?"

She maintained that perplexing silence.

"Lookee here," Aunt Hattie called out.

Detective Loach was descending the stairs.

"Here comes de judge," Aunt Hattie announced.

Loach walked over slowly and stopped in front of Lucy.

"I'll take your statement now," he told her.

"Fine. But my aunt Hattie needs something to eat. Can she be excused for a few hours?"

Lucy didn't wait for Loach's reply. She turned to me.

"Markus, do you know that inexpensive steak place on Eighty-sixth Street?"

"Yes. The Embers. Or something like that."

"Will you please take Aunt Hattie there now and give her some sustenance. She needs to keep up her strength. I'll come join you after I consult with Detective Loach. The poor man needs all the help he can get."

Detective Loach, in response, decided to give Lucy a curt little lecture.

"I have no problem with that. But just remember that your aunt is going to be questioned by the D.A.'s office. They may or may not go to the grand jury. If they go, the odds are against indictment. They never indict in a Good Samaritan scenario. She came upon a crime in progress. She interceded to save your friend, who was being attacked by a shovel-wielding perp. But the weapons charge is going to be dealt with. In other words, just make sure your aunt is available."

"Aunt Hattie is always available," Lucy noted.

"Thank you, dearie," Aunt Hattie said.

Five minutes later we were standing in line in the cafeteria-style steak joint.

An enormous man in a ridiculous chef's outfit stood by the flaming grill and called out, "What'll you have?"

I read off all the listings on the wall menu to Aunt

Hattie. Four kinds of steaks. Chicken. Shrimp. Ribs. Burgers. Or any combination thereof.

She seemed deep in thought. Then she asked, "What are you having, Marco?"

"Markus," I corrected. "I'm not having anything right now. I'm not hungry."

She thought again.

"I'll have pork chops," she finally announced.

"We don't have pork chops," the man by the grill said.

"Then give me just one."

"One what?"

"Pork chop."

"Lady, I just told you. We don't serve pork chops."

"He doesn't have pork chops," I confirmed, trying to edge her away from a close encounter with the grill man.

"I don't like these fancy places," Hattie said.

She settled for a sirloin steak, a baked potato, a piece of garlic bread, and a glass of ginger ale.

We sat down in a booth. She took her hat off, studied it, then placed it deliberately down beside her.

I watched her first eat the steak, then the potato, then the bread. She left not a single piece of gristle, skin, or crust on the plate.

The plate was so clean it bounced the ceiling lights around the booth like a reflector.

Then she drank the entire glass of ginger ale.

Then, before I could stop her, she took out a pack of Viceroy cigarettes, shook one loose, and lit it—inhaling deeply.

"You're not allowed to smoke here," I said, "nor in any other restaurant in New York."

Her eyes narrowed angrily. She snubbed the cigarette out on her plate.

"Well, let's not beat around the damn bush anymore, Marco."

I hadn't the slightest idea what she was talking about, so I said, "I want to thank you for saving my life in the park."

"Don't be changing the subject."

"What subject?"

She leaned over and said, "I figure we can talk real straight. No razzle-dazzle. You and me have been sitting on the same log for the same amount of time."

The woman obviously was telling me that she and I were the same age. That was absurd. She had to be about twenty years older than I. Did I really look that old?

"I will talk straight with you," I said.

"Good. Now, doing right by Lucy is important. The poor girl always got confused about a lot of things. People take advantage of her. I told her to buy some land and sit on it. No, she comes to the big city and starts messing around with books. You know what I mean. Poor Lucy goes into a store to buy some buttons and she comes out all happy with hard-boiled eggs. See?"

"What makes you think I'm not doing right by Lucy?"

"Just checking up."

"Listen, I've loved her from the first moment I met her."

"What are your intentions, Marco?"

Oh, my God! My intentions? If Lucy ever heard this conversation she would crawl under the table. Or would she?

"Honorable," I replied.

"So you say."

"Well, what kind of proof do you want?" I exploded. "Look at me. Do I look like some kind of Don Juan? Do I look like a fortune hunter? Do I look like a hypersexed seducer?"

"You snarl at me, Marco, and you'll get snookered."

"I didn't mean to raise my voice. I'm sorry."

"Play the fool, pay the fool, Marco."

"Wait. Let's start over."

"Good. You're not as dumb as you look, Marco."

"Markus," I corrected.

"And I'm no dummy, either," she said.

"Of course not."

"But I heard about you people."

"What people?"

"Italians and such."

"I'm not Italian. My father was a French Jew and my mother a Greek folksinger."

"Don't matter. I like you people, but I heard. I heard you think all of us are stupid."

She reached over and poked her finger into my shoulder, hard, three times, saying, "Like those fools who were going to bury a rattler in a box."

"What rattler? What box?"

"In the park."

"You mean tonight?"

"Yep. Now *they* was stupid."

The conversation, if one could call it that, had taken an intriguing turn. I was curious.

"Why were they trying to bury the snake? Is that what one does in those snake-handling ceremonies?"

"Hell, no. That wasn't no ceremony there, Marco. That wasn't no prayer meeting. Hell, there wasn't even a tambourine. Man, where's your eyes?"

"What *were* they doing, then?"

"Cleaning up. Closing down. Moving out. But they don't know nothing. You don't get rid of rattlers by burying 'em live in wooden boxes. You can put the box eighty feet down in God's own earth and some of them are getting out."

"That's why he had a shovel in his hand," I said quietly, as if I had made a profound discovery.

In fact, I was absolutely floored by the realization that I had stumbled upon the gathering just as they were disbanding their operations. It had simply never dawned on me.

And then came another realization. Lucy's brilliant analysis was missing so many important elements that it just didn't make sense. Except to fools.

"Speakin' of the devil," Aunt Hattie said happily.

I turned and saw that Lucy had entered the restaurant and was standing in the steak line.

A saying of my father's—may he rest in peace—suddenly popped into my head: If you believe in luck, you might as well believe you can get a crease in your pants without ironing them.

Aunt Hattie and I waited in silence for Lucy. She

arrived at the booth with a small sirloin, an ear of corn, a salad, and a large cup of water.

She sat next to me, facing her aunt.

"Don't like the looks of that one," Aunt Hattie said, pointing to Lucy's steak. "Don't like the way it lays there."

"Is everything okay?" Lucy asked.

Aunt Hattie just grumbled. I stared straight ahead.

Lucy cut a small piece of steak, topped it with a smaller piece of tomato, and chewed it thoughtfully. She swallowed.

Then she said, "You look pale again, Markus. Is something bothering you? Or is it just fatigue? Poor man. What a long day it has been for you. Have you eaten?"

"No. I didn't eat. Yes, I am exhausted. And yes, something is bothering me."

"Well, speak up."

"I want to talk to you alone, Lucy."

"I have no secrets from Aunt Hattie."

"Thank you, dearie," the old lady said, smirking in triumph,

"Look, Lucy! A lot of things suddenly don't make sense."

"Yes?"

"Did you know that they were closing up shop?"

"Who?"

"The rattlesnake worshippers."

"They weren't rattlesnake worshippers, Markus. They were Christians who pick up poisonous snakes."

"It doesn't matter what they were. Did you know?"

"Let's say I had an inkling."

"And you knew the exact location of their church, didn't you?"

"Well, as I told you, that watercolor of the Eaglevale Bridge by Harlow Trent showed—"

I cut her off, almost savagely, with a chopping movement of my hand through the air.

"You weren't really lost, were you, Lucy?"

"Markus," she said gently, "my steak is getting cold."

The fury boiled up in me.

"You set me up, didn't you? You've been manipulating me like a puppet. All the time, from the very beginning. Oh, Lucy! How could you?"

"What do you want, Markus!"

"Answers, damn it! I want answers."

She smiled.

"Tomorrow morning, Markus, I'm taking Aunt Hattie bird-watching. Now, that's the time for answers, isn't it, Markus? Be there."

Was the woman mad? Birding in the morning as if nothing had happened.

But then the fatigue rolled over me like a fog. I could not speak. I could not protest. I just sat there and stared at Lucy's steak.

Chapter 15

I slept the sleep of the just—seven strong hours.

I awoke feeling like a frisky, ravenous forty-year-old.

At six-thirty that morning I walked across the street and had a huge poppy seed bagel with scallion cream cheese and a café au lait. Then a regular coffee.

Then, dressed in faded blue madras pants, a washed-out print sport shirt, and a pair of high-top sneakers, I headed for the rendezvous.

It was a glorious morning, a bird-watcher's dream. Plenty of sun, very little humidity, and a caressing breeze.

But of course I wasn't going there to watch birds. I was going there for good old-fashioned enlightenment.

When I reached the rendezvous point just inside the park at Ninetieth Street, Lucy, Aunt Hattie, and John Wu were already assembled.

It was the first time I had seen Aunt Hattie in the light of the day. The family resemblance to Lucy was evident but the night and the artificial light of the precinct had muted her—how should I put it delicately?—her specifics.

She was heavier than Lucy; not fat, just rawboned.

She had the same thin neck as Lucy, but it was longer, much longer.

Her face was deeper than Lucy's . . . sort of like an antelope's . . . designed for long-distance gazing over flat plains.

Her hair was an astonishing jumble of gray and brown and just a hint of red.

She carried her hat now, and the strong wrist of the hand that held the hat was encompassed, nay, enveloped, by an old-fashioned wristwatch of gigantic proportions.

Aunt Hattie wore a faded housedress that buttoned up the front, and under it a frazzled sweater. There was, of course, no need for such a sweater on that mild day.

Her shoes were a wonder . . . they actually were rope sandals with wood platform heels.

"You forgot your binoculars again, Markus," Lucy said, in lieu of a greeting.

"Sorry," was all I could muster in reply.

John Wu gave me a little sneer. It was what he expected of me.

Then we saw Peter Marin approaching with his rolling gait, like a large barrel picking up speed down a bumpy slope.

When he reached us, he looked around wildly.

"Where's Emma?"

I looked quickly at Lucy. Lucy looked off into the distance.

John Wu said, "Who knows? And where's Beatrice?"

The absence of Emma seemed to derange poor Peter. His eyes began to distend and he kept wiping his brow and neck with a sleeve.

I empathized with him. After all, I, too, had fallen under her spell. But at least my infatuation had miraculously turned up key evidence in the murder of Abraham Lescalles.

"She'll come," said Peter with dogged but nervous optimism.

We all waited, watching the joggers enter and leave the park, watching the ducks and gulls noisily rising and falling above the nearby reservoir.

"Oh, my, Peter. Forgive me!" Lucy suddenly burst out. "I forgot to introduce you. This is my aunt Hattie. Aunt Hattie, this is Peter Marin. A wonderful man and a birder without peer."

Peter gave what could only be described as an awkward bow.

Aunt Hattie sort of grunted.

We waited.

"What time do you have, Aunt Hattie?" Lucy asked.

The old woman held up the huge watch. It read three minutes past seven.

"Why don't I call Emma?" an increasingly desperate Peter suggested. "And someone else can call Beatrice."

John Wu gave him a contemptuous stare. Peter, embarrassed, looked away.

As well he should; even I knew that no self-respecting bird-watcher would make such a call.

The code was clear and rigid. Those who show—go. Those who don't—don't.

I wondered why Lucy didn't just tell Peter and John what had happened. They'd learn about it soon enough.

Maybe, I thought, her silence on the matter was just another weird bird-watching tradition: nothing should get in the way of the day's outing.

Or maybe it was that Lucy felt Peter and John would not believe her . . . they simply were incapable of believing that Emma Pip and Beatrice Plumb participated in a murderous rattlesnake cult, albeit of a Christian persuasion.

"We'll wait another two minutes," Lucy announced.

"Let's give them ten minutes," Peter replied.

"No. Two. I'm taking my aunt to the Sink first; I think we should get moving."

"Good idea," said John Wu.

"It'll remind her of home," Lucy said.

Aunt Hattie gave her niece a sour look.

But there was now a more upbeat atmosphere in our little group. Everyone, and I mean everyone, loved to go to the Sink. It was a small piece of swamp in the Ramble, bordered on one side by a small "finger" of lakefront and on the other by high rock outcroppings.

The Sink was filled with enormous willows and willow oaks growing every which way but straight. This mix of rock and muck and lake and trees seemed like a romanticized derelict garden constructed by a psychotic genius. But it was the life-forms in the Sink that dazzled the most. It had become a kind of primeval soup.

There were thrushes, finches, warblers, flycatchers, and sparrows.

There were screaming blue jays and morbid crows.

Yet birds were only a small part of the intensity.

There were water rats and land rats. Moles and voles. Squirrels and chipmunks.

What about the frogs? Plenty of them. And bass rising. And snapping turtles. All of them feeding on the beetles and dragonflies and butterflies, not to mention those strange stilt-legged mosquitoes which hung like bats on the sides of rocks.

Yes. The Sink was wonderful. But most birders had stopped going there regularly. It had assumed a kind of spiritual quality, where no one should use a camera, lift a pair of binoculars, record a species.

It had become a place of repose and mystery . . . a derelict garden that was without any function at all except to be there.

At six minutes after seven, Lucy shot Peter Marin one of her stern looks. It meant the Olmsted's Irregulars were about to shove off. And he had to fish or cut bait.

We started walking. He hesitated for only a moment and then joined the line of march.

Ten brisk minutes later we stood on the rocks above the Sink.

A green heron had stepped into view, wading daintily in the muck of the far side.

We all knew there were two breeding pairs of green herons now in the park. But this one seemed a stranger, a new arrival. He looked like he had been heading for Connecticut and got lost.

Aunt Hattie said something to Lucy, who laughed.

Lucy then called out, "My aunt Hattie says the heron is so beautiful it gives her a stomachache."

"It is the way we think they move and the way we think they don't move," said the ever analytical and often cryptic John Wu. "Herons appear to do everything in the most exquisite slow motion. But then you realize that they really move very fast."

I nodded agreement with John even though I didn't see the slightest connection with what Aunt Hattie had said and felt.

Then I made a signal to Lucy that it was time for us to converse.

She nodded and moved uplake along the rock cliff, to a kind of lonesome promontory.

I meandered over and joined her.

"You hear the downy woodpeckers?" she asked.

"No."

"Listen! They're in that glade on the other side of the Sink."

"Don't start that nonsense again," I barked.

"What nonsense, Markus?" she asked innocently.

"You know. Like you did last night on our stroll. All that 'music of the birds' nonsense. The harpsichord. The rustling of the wings. You know!"

"My, my, aren't you grumpy this morning."

"I want no more subterfuge, Lucy."

"Then you shall have none, my dear Markus. Not one shred."

I had a sudden desire to kiss her, passionately. But I restrained myself. First things first.

"You were not lost in the park last night, Lucy."

"Correct, Markus. I was not lost."

"It was simply a ploy to get me to that Eaglevale Bridge."

"Correct."

"I was almost killed."

"There was little real danger, Markus. Aunt Hattie was on duty."

"How did you know they were there—that night?"

"Sheila Ott and her terrace telescope. I recruited her as an observer after I discovered the hidden chamber in the watercolor. She was happy to help after I suggested to her the real cause of her sister's death. She signaled me from her building with a flashlight. It was clearly visible across the park where we were."

"Did you know they were in the process of disbanding the church . . . getting rid of the snakes . . . closing up shop?"

"I did," she replied.

I took a deep breath. A breeze hit me gently in the face. There were always breezes in the rocks above the Sink.

"How did you know?" I asked.

"Your package of raw liver with the baby rattle frightened them. The baby rattle was too close to a snake's rattle. It was a sign to them that their secret had been exposed."

"But, Lucy, it had to be they who sent the package

of liver to me. Just as it was they who threw those two other packages through your window, to warn you against further investigation."

"Ah, dear Markus! They threw the packages through my window for the reason stated. But they didn't deliver that final package."

"Who did?"

"I did."

My legs became a bit weak. Her audacity was beyond belief.

"Why?"

"I knew that some members of the snake-handling church were birders. But other than Emma Pip, I had no inkling who they were. So I sent you the package, knowing that you would show up with it in the park. If you recall, I made a point of displaying the contents of the package to both bird-watching groups. The trick . . . the trap . . . worked quite well. They lost their nerve. That set the stage for your brave confrontation with them. Of course I turned out to be quite wrong in regard to Paula Fox."

"Why did you suspect Emma?"

"Her sudden appearance out of nowhere was just too suspicious. It was obvious she was looking for information. She was looking to find out how much I knew. Besides, she had that wild streak in her . . . a streak that is often found in snake handlers. Anyway, this is why I brought the two of you together."

"What are you talking about? You brought Emma and me together?"

"Yes. I sensed you were sweet on her. And I knew

she wanted to know you, for different reasons. So I set it up."

"You mean that the whole thing about not wanting to see me anymore . . . that whole fake story about a man named Duke who turned out to be a dog . . . it was all just another devious plot?"

"I'm afraid so, Markus. But it did turn out well, didn't it? You gathered some valuable information while you were playing games."

"It's ugly as hell, Lucy. I was a damn marionette and I didn't know who was pulling the strings."

"Yes, you could say that. But there are more flattering ways to describe what happened. And of course Emma herself was probably being manipulated by Beatrice, who needed a spy in the nerve center of Olmsted's Irregulars."

"The idea of Beatrice Plumb as a spymaster or snake handler is very hard to swallow. I just can't comprehend it."

"Keep trying, Markus."

"One last thing, Lucy."

"What?"

"When did Aunt Hattie show up?"

"Forty-eight hours ago. But we kept in touch."

"What do you mean, 'kept in touch'? "

"Remember my last trip to Chapel Hill?"

"Yes."

"I went there to visit friends after we gave up the investigation?"

"Yes."

"Well, I didn't go to Chapel Hill."

"What?"

"I went home to consult with Aunt Hattie."

"Why did you lie to me?"

"To protect you, Markus."

"From what?"

"I had deduced the existence of a murderous snake-handling cult by that time."

Then I exploded.

"How could you! You didn't say a word to me. And besides, there wasn't a clue."

"On the contrary, Markus. There were three very important clues."

"Like what?"

"The glove."

"What glove?"

"The glove we found among Abraham's hidden belongings. It is the kind handlers often use when they're transporting snakes."

I had forgotten all about the glove. Now I remembered it and I remembered that Aunt Hattie had used something like it when she had pulled the rattler out of its box and scared me half to death.

"And don't forget the knife, Markus."

"Ah, that homemade knife."

"Yes. It turns out to be the kind of knife poachers use down home."

"Poachers?"

"Men and women who supplement their income by illegally killing rattlesnakes. There's good money in the venom and the skins. It was Abraham's knife. And he probably obtained the knife when he was down South obtaining the snakes."

"On his fake camping trips, you mean."

"Exactly."

There was a sudden commotion among the birders. And then it died down.

It seemed that Aunt Hattie's stomachache caused by the green heron's beauty had become so acute that she had flung a stone at said bird.

Whereupon Peter Marin had chastised her, and almost got his head bitten off because she didn't appreciate his chastisement.

"And finally, Markus, there was the Gospel."

"Which Gospel?"

"The Gospel of Mark. Remember our visit to the Episcopalian priest who knew Abraham?"

"Yes."

"That was the key that tied the glove and the knife together. It was obvious that Abraham was fascinated by the Gospel of Mark. A very deep fascination for a layman. Yes! But perfectly logical when you know that the only commandment to pick up poisonous snakes in the Bible—for some sort of spiritual redemption—appears at the close of Mark's Gospel. While virtually all biblical scholars today consider those lines a very late addition, Abraham considered them sacred text. He believed in that commandment. When he lost his faith, he died for it."

"Your aunt recited those passages to me the other night."

"She handled snakes when she was a young woman. In a snake-handling church. Her second husband died in such a church."

"My God, Lucy! I didn't know!"

"But not from snakebite. From drinking battery acid."

"Are you serious?"

"Don't you remember that part of the text, Markus? 'If they drink any deadly thing, it shall not hurt them.' "

"What a horror!"

Lucy smiled sweetly. She said, "There are many rooms in the house of the Lord."

"And the whole fourth floor is filled with loonies."

"Be compassionate, Markus. And stop using the word 'loony.' It offends all of us who love the common loon. "

I didn't reply. We stood there for a long while, not saying another word.

Then, Lucy came close to me and placed both her hands around the back of my neck, like she was about to scold me.

"Are you still angry with me, Markus?"

"I don't think so."

"Good. I can't stand it when you're angry like that."

"I'm hurt but I'm not angry."

She kissed me on the forehead. Lucy is taller than I, so she had to bend a bit.

"I should have consulted you more," she admitted. "And I apologize."

"You're forgiven."

"And, after all, it was both of us working together who solved the murder of Abraham Lescalles."

"Yes, I suppose it was."

"When all is said and done, Markus, we worked as a team. When you hunted, I guarded the nest. When I hunted, you watched the brood. Like that red-tailed hawk family high on the Fifth Avenue building."

"I guess you can look at it that way, Lucy."

"But we aren't finished yet. Are we, Markus? Another few steps to go."

This got my attention.

"Steps? What steps?"

"There's one more crime we have to solve."

"Who? Where?"

"It's a case so perplexing, so fraught with danger, that I shudder even contemplating it."

"Tell me, Lucy!"

"Who killed Cock Robin?"

And then she burst into laughter at her own Mother Goose joke.

I was tolerant. After all, Lucy rarely made any jokes at all.

We headed back toward the main group.

"Wait a moment," Lucy said.

We stopped.

"I was making a joke about finding out who killed Cock Robin."

"I assumed that."

"But I am quite serious about the plight of the American robin."

"What plight? The park is full of them."

"But bird-watchers have abandoned them. They don't even look at robins anymore. Robins have become like pigeons."

"I agree with you there."

"But it's not fair, Markus. The robin is an extraordinary creature."

"Okay."

"We should do something to help it recover its reputation."

"That would be hard, Lucy. By the time a bird-watcher reaches adulthood, he or she is sick to death of robin redbreast."

"Yes, I understand. But the robin is a terribly complex bird."

"I take your word for it."

"Did you know, Markus, that ounce for ounce it is the most efficient predator on the planet?"

"I didn't know. But I assume the worms know."

"Am I talking strangely, Markus?" she asked. Her face was so lovely and pale. Her hands were nervous, one plucking her headband, the other fiddling with the strap of her binoculars. Ah, in a sense, Lucy was always unpredictable. One moment she was crushing me with the weight of her elegant logic and the next moment she was a white-haired child.

She said, "I just don't know why I suddenly thought of robins with such intensity."

"It's been a very difficult few days, Lucy. We are all acting strangely."

"Markus, look! At Aunt Hattie! She's put her hat on!"

I looked. Indeed she had. So what?

But it obviously meant something to Lucy, who was rushing back.

That is the story of my life with Lucy Wayles. She always sees something I don't see.

I didn't see Lucy for the next six days.

She kept me informed of developments by telephone.

The doorman, Nolan, did indeed confess to being present at the murder of Abraham Lescalles. But he claimed that Emma and Beatrice had actually wielded the knife. And he claimed that he had tried to stop them.

In exchange for his confession, the charges of assault against me were dropped.

Lucy had been absolutely right as to motive, also. According to Nolan, Lescalles had indeed lost his "faith" and was about to disclose the circumstances surrounding the death of Sylvia Rand.

It turned out that there were only two other parishioners in the snake-handling church. Neither of them was implicated in the murder. One of them, in fact, was a park maintenance worker.

It turned out that Emma Pip was the daughter of a man who had helped Abraham Lescalles set up a homeless-feeding program at the Church of the Heavenly Dove.

It turned out that the district attorney's office declined to press any charges whatsoever against Aunt Hattie.

On the seventh day at four o'clock in the afternoon, the downstairs buzzer rang.

It was the security man in the lobby. Two women were here to see me.

"Send them up!" I ordered.

I waited just outside the door, in the hallway, listening to the elevator ascend.

Out came Lucy and Aunt Hattie, carrying luggage.

Lucy gave me a very formal "How nice to see you again, Markus" and then kissed me on the cheek as if I were the husband of her second cousin who had just got out of a hospital.

All Aunt Hattie did was nearly knock me over getting into the apartment.

"Don't like hallways," she muttered. "Don't like people who keep me waiting in hallways."

Once inside, we sat down on chairs around a coffee table.

Aunt Hattie stared around boldly.

"How many people live here?"

"Just me."

She shook her head disapprovingly, leaned forward, and stared down the hall along which the bedrooms lay.

"How many rooms?"

"Six."

She exhaled censoriously and adjusted her hat.

"I hope your niece will live here one day with me, as my wife," I said, half proudly, half hopefully.

"Don't hold your breath," she muttered.

I looked to Lucy for help, but all she said was, "We can't stay long. Aunt Hattie is making a five-thirty bus at Port Authority."

"Home?"

"Yes."

"Aunt Hattie likes buses," Lucy said.

Aunt Hattie lit one of her Viceroys. I dug up an ashtray fast and then brought out a bowl with two bananas, a tangerine, and two apples in it.

Aunt Hattie stared at the fruit like it was from another galaxy.

"How is your health?" Lucy suddenly asked me.

"I think my health is excellent," I replied.

"Good. People our age can't be too careful . . . can we, Markus?"

"I guess not."

Suddenly, one of the pieces of luggage began to move.

I stared incredulously.

Then I realized I was looking at a cat carrier.

Did Aunt Hattie travel with a cat? What was going on?

Then the carrier subsided. I realized it hadn't really moved; it had just shaken from side to side.

"He used to be a fine physician," I heard Lucy say to her aunt, apropos of me. Then she added, "But he just doesn't take care of himself properly. Not since he retired."

"I can imagine."

"And he's often lonely. Oh, there is *me*, Aunt Hattie. I'm with him a lot."

Lucy leaned over and put her hand on my head, as if she were about to tousle a little boy's hair.

"But he leads a lonely existence. Sometimes, Aunt Hattie, he walks the streets for hours. Oh, he has become a tolerable enough birder. But his heart is really elsewhere."

"Poor man," said Aunt Hattie.

"You have grown fond of him, haven't you?"

"Sure!"

It was the strangest conversation they were having, about me, in my presence.

I was being set up for something. I could feel it. Maybe they wanted me to accompany them to the bus terminal.

Before I could speculate further, it happened.

Lucy kissed me, almost passionately.

Aunt Hattie walked over to the cat carrier and opened it.

Lucy rushed over to the carrier and pulled something out.

Aunt Hattie shut the carrier.

The two came toward me.

I sat back in my chair, aghast.

Lucy was holding a small dog in her arms.

It wasn't just any dog. It was Duke. The three-legged pit bull.

"No!" I cried.

"He needs a home, Markus," she replied.

Lucy, Hattie, and Duke were now beside the coffee table, only a few inches away from me.

It was too late for flight.

"Everyone needs a home, Lucy. No!"

"He loves you, Markus."

"He'll get over it."

And them she pushed—I could almost say threw—the beast into my lap.

I stared into his quite ugly face. He sort of smiled.

"They don't allow dogs in this building," I fairly screamed.

"Now they do. Believe me," said Lucy.

She whipped out a piece of paper.

"Listen carefully, Markus. Here's what he eats. Are you listening?"

"Please, Lucy."

"He is not allowed to have fruit, eggs, milk products, chocolate, pasta, lamb, or goat. He can eat beef, chicken, pork, and any dry dog food. As for turkey, the situation is unclear. Supplement with chopped greens."

She folded the paper and placed it under the ashtray I had secured for Aunt Hattie.

"Lucy, have mercy. I can't do this."

The three-legged Duke suddenly rolled over onto his back.

And he was staring at me!

Duke was very stumpy. Very muscular. Very threatening.

He looked like the canine equivalent of those one-legged veterans at parades who sell red poppies.

"Now, there are a few other things you have to know, Markus."

Aunt Hattie had started to pull the rest of the luggage toward the door.

"He's kind and gentle, Markus. But you mustn't provoke him."

"Why would I do that?"

"You might do it without thinking. Like just switching on the radio or TV. You mustn't do that."

"Why?"

"He attacks radios and TVs when they're on, three legs and all. Don't ask me why. I don't know. Just don't play them."

Aunt Hattie yelled out, "Marco, that dog can hunt! Lucy! It's time!"

"One last thing, Markus. Don't worry. He understands English perfectly."

She kissed me again and whispered in my ear. "You can get him a prosthetic device if you wish."

And then they were gone.

For twenty minutes I sat there, absolutely still.

Duke kept staring me. Once in a while I stared back. It was very uncomfortable.

What does one do with a three-legged pit bull who is kind and gentle but attacks radios and TVs once they're turned on, regardless of the quality of the program?

And what did Lucy mean when she said that Duke understands English? Did she mean it literally?

I waited. Something had to give sooner or later.

Finally, I broached the subject.

"Duke, could you get off me?"

He didn't appear to understand my request. He stayed where he was. But I did hear a distant sound from the pit of his stomach. A primal growl? Or was it a moan of grief?

The phone rang. I picked it up dexterously so as not to jar Duke.

It was Lucy.

"Everything's fine here, Markus. Aunt Hattie will be boarding in about five minutes."

"That's nice."

"And how is everything there?"

"Not too good."

"What's the matter?"

"I can't seem to get Duke off me."

"Where are you? Where is Duke?"

"On the chair."

"You mean the same chair you were in when we left? You mean you haven't moved?"

"Correct."

"Are you afraid of him, Markus?"

"Yes."

"Put him on the phone."

"He's a dog, Lucy. Dogs don't use phones."

"Just put the receiver by his ear."

I did so.

A second later, Duke hopped off, made a perfect three-point landing, and shuffled down the hall and into one of the bedrooms.

"What did you say to him, Lucy? What did you say?"

Lucy replied. "I told him to beware the tufted duck."

Then she added, "Tomorrow morning! Seven A.M., Markus. The Olmsted's Irregulars. We're bloody but unbowed. And don't forget your binoculars this time."

She hung up. I wondered if I was supposed to furnish Duke with pajamas.

I snoozed for about five minutes.

Then I walked down the hall and into Duke's new bedroom.

The beast seemed to be musing on the floor, utterly content. His beady eyes followed me.

"Let's get a few things straight," I said.

He closed his eyes.

"I know you are physically challenged, but . . ."

My heart did a little flip-flop for the poor doggie. But then I caught myself. The riot act had to be read.

"Okay. Listen. I may be Lucy Wayles's puppet but I'm not going to be yours. Lucy is beautiful. Lucy is wonderful. I love Lucy. You are just a temporary boarder and you're not paying rent. Remember the sun dance of the Sioux nation? Remember the ceremonial dish served at the sun dance? Let me refresh your canine memory. It was always stewed puppy and wild turnips."

I let that sink into his thick head for a few minutes, and then walked back to the living room.

I felt much better. Lucy once told me, when I first met her, "Remember, Markus, both flamingos and mustard bite."

When I asked her what that really meant, she had replied sweetly, "I don't know, Markus. Lewis Carroll said it."

Now I had an inkling what it meant. I could bite like a pit bull if I chose to.

I selected a book from the shelf and sat down.

It was titled *Birds of the Atlantic Shore*. It was subtitled *From the Keys to the Maritimes*.

I opened the book to the introduction, written by an ornithologist at the University of Delaware.

I would, I realized, do anything to impress Lucy Wayles.

Don't miss the next book in the
Lucy Wayles Series,

*Beware the
Butcher-Bird,*

Coming to you from Signet
in May 1997

It was 6:31 P.M. on the second Tuesday in November. The first truly cold day of autumn.

I stood before the old wood-framed full-length mirror in my bedroom, inspecting my appearance and knotting my tie—slowly, carefully.

I am hardly anyone's idea of a clotheshorse. But that night I was taking pains with my appearance. The tie I was fussing over was brand-new, only three hours old in fact. I acquired it at one of the snootier men's stores on Madison Avenue. And I had spent an absolutely outrageous sixty-eight dollars on it. Plus tax. All to impress my ladylove, Miss Lucy Wayles.

It *was* a lovely tie, if a little audacious. Deep brown silk with lighter brown herons dancing down its length in a pretty pattern.

Yes, I simply had to impress Lucy, and goodness knows I'd have gone a lot further than purchasing an overpriced cravat to do it.

When I was satisfied that the knot was perfect, I stepped back to take in my total image.

Oh.

I was still rather short. Still a geriatric Romeo. I had not been transformed into a matinee idol.

No matter. I felt wonderful anyway. I was escorting Lucy to a gala dinner that night. All our bird-watching colleagues would be in attendance as well. It was going to be a grand evening. And why not? The morning had been just as grand.

Lucy had led us into the park at 7:00 A.M., as usual—"us" being the Olmsted's Irregulars, bird-watchers without peer.

Actually, we were not an old, established bird-watching group. We were relatively new. Lucy Wayles, the president and founder, had split us off from the parent group—the Central Park Bird-watchers—because of, as she put it, "severe ideological differences."

In fact, Lucy had been asked in less than polite terms to leave the parent group a little over a year ago. She had been arrested for holding up traffic on the Fifty-ninth Street Bridge during her daring high-wire rescue of a wayward tufted duck. If not for her efforts, the frightened creature would surely have frozen to death. It had been something of a media event. Lucy even made the six o'clock news.

But the Central Park Bird-watchers had found her actions less than dignified. Lucy's heroics were definitely not the kind of attention the group appreciated. Some of the group members had had words with Lucy. And needless to say, she had some choice words for them. One thing led to another. And the end result was the founding of our little splinter group.

Olmsted's Irregulars (named, of course, after the genius who designed Central Park) originally con-

sisted of Lucy, myself, Peter Marin, John Wu, Emma
Pip, and Beatrice Plumb.

Alas, two of these individuals were no longer
among our number. Indeed, they were now doing their
birding from prison yards upstate, after a most com-
plicated series of events led them to participate in a
gruesome murder—all of which I have detailed elsewhere.

At any rate, the Irregulars had recently picked up a
new member: Willa Wayne, a young woman—forty
being quite young by my standards—who gave every
indication of being a sterling addition to our group.
She was lively and intelligent and very pretty and, it
seemed, quite well off. It seemed that every garment
she owned, even the short pants and rugby shirts she
often wore for bird-watching, had been purchased at
the very poshest of the designer boutiques in town.

Ms. Wayne had not exactly been forthcoming about
her personal life. She told us that she was married to a
violinist with the New York Philharmonic, but as yet
she had not disclosed his name.

Our first stop that morning was the reservoir.

Nothing unusual there—laughing gulls and ducks,
canvasbacks, greater and lesser scaups, and buffle-
heads.

In a little while we moved on to the Ramble—that
expanse of wooded beauty where the city and all its
cares seemed to fall and fade away. You could not
glimpse a single skyscraper or hear a single taxicab's
horn from the depths of the Ramble. It was like a
country glade right in the middle of Manhattan.

By night, of course, the story was quite different.

Things went on in that sylvan glade that were the stuff of nightmares. Things that only the birds would know about.

It was there in the Ramble that we came upon three red-bellied woodpeckers cavorting on a very old pin oak.

Not redheaded woodpeckers, mind you! These were red-*bellied* woodpeckers, which are rare in Central Park. And they were keeping up a fearsome racket that sounded very like the mad mariachi section in a Latin mambo band.

It sounded something like: *chuh . . . chuc-chuh . . . chow-chow . . . cherr-cherr*.

And sometimes: *chawh-chawh!!*

They were also making all kinds of strange moves in syncopation with their song: raising their crests; spreading wings and tails; bowing. It was something to see!

Their backs and rumps were conspicuously barred in black and white—transversely. Their underparts were gray. Their wings were spotted or barred with white. And what appeared to be their vaunted red bellies were really only reddish tinges on their abdomens.

I thought I head John Wu mumble something.

"What was that?" I asked him.

"An irregular wanderer," John announced scornfully, lip cured.

He was referring to the birds, surely, not me. And I assumed he meant that the red-bellied woodpecker does not have a regular migration pattern.

Well, John was seldom wrong about such things.

But so what? Why was the humble woodpecker's migration pattern a subject for his contempt?

John was a fairly strange bird himself. But it would never occur to me to question or challenge him. His knowledge of the avian world was vast, while mine was minuscule. And he was a respected investment counselor working in a dynamic business atmosphere, while I was a superannuated retired physician whose specialty had been research on the virus that causes the common cold. Not terribly glamorous, is it?

I turned my attention back to the dancing birds. John Wu's scorn notwithstanding, I rather admired them for their irregularity; but, at my age, the incongruities in life seemed so much more interesting than the predictable patterns.

We watched a while longer. As I looked at the woodpeckers, I began to feel an almost overwhelming sadness.

You see, they reminded me of our two incarcerated comrades. (They had a coconspirator in their crimes who wasn't a bird-watcher.)

The birds looked like convicts in the prison yard haggling over a smoke.

I cast a quick and furtive glance at burly Peter Marin. Apparently he had not picked up on the connection. Still, I tried to keep an eye on poor Peter. He had been devastated by the whole affair. I honestly doubt that he will ever recover from it.

By and by, the woodpeckers left us.

During our morning break one of those inevitable arguments broke out. Such altercations are unfailingly heated, but at the same time they seem to invigorate the arguing birders no end. In truth, bird-watchers would rather fight than eat.

This time the argument was between Peter and the new member, Willa Wayne.

Willa said, speaking of the departed woodpeckers, "Those birds are obvious psychotics. Obvious. This is not the season for courtship rituals."

Whereupon Peter Marin replied, "I beg to differ with you. That was not courtship behavior we just witnessed."

"Are you blind? Of course it was," Willa countered indignantly. She had a long, thin face and when she turned those black dagger eyes upon you it was just as if you were being pinned to velvet like a prize butterfly.

"The courtship behavior of the red-bellied woodpecker," Peter spat out venomously, "is characterized by mutual tapping and reverse mounting. Period. It's textbook stuff, madam."

"Does anybody have any salt?"

It was Lucy who had interrupted the fight with that innocuous question. She was holding a shelled hard-boiled egg.

We all began to search our backpacks for salt.

And the argument was forgotten.

Once again, Lucy had displayed her leadership qualities.

Yes, all in all, a very good morning.

When I finished dressing I walked into Duke's bedroom to get his opinion.

No, I do not have a roommate. Not exactly. Let me

explain: Duke is a three-legged pit bull who—how shall I put it?—came into my life recently.

He was foisted upon me by Lucy and her crazy down-home aunt Hattie—who is wont to wander around Manhattan with a loaded shotgun.

Duke doesn't like me particularly, but I value his opinions, when he cares to express them—which is not often.

The beast was in his favorite spot, on the rug, surrounded by dozens of rawhide bones, which Lucy keeps sending him.

Duke likes holding one of them in his teeth when we go for a walk.

People on the street, seeing this pit bull hip-hopping along on three legs with a bone in his jaws, just don't know what to say or do or think. One lady walked over to me, keeping clear of Duke, handed me a five-dollar bill, and whispered: "Why don't you buy this poor dog a real bone?"

I stood in the middle of Duke's room, striking a pose with my coat draped over one arm. "Well, what do you think?"

The beady-eyed bugger groaned, got up, and hobbled around to the other side of the bed, out of sight.

I could hear him plop down again.

"Thank you, Duke," I said pleasantly. "That will be all for now."

I took the elevator down, nodded good evening to the doorman, and headed toward the Hilton. It was a short walk from my Fifty-seventh Street apartment to the hotel.

I looked at my watch. It was 7:03.

Lucy had set the time of arrival for seven-fifteen. We were all to meet then, across from the Hilton, in the small park at Fifty-fourth Street.

Lucy said a preliminary meeting was necessary because the award dinner might become so boring so fast that a rational escape plan must be drawn up.

Why the dinner? And what was the award? All the Irregulars had asked those questions when Lucy first informed us of the festivities.

A number of environmental and wildlife groups—including Audubon, Sierra Club, and Nature Conservancy—had formed a kind of consortium to create the Conservationist of the Year medal. Tonight would be the first presentation of the honor, and it was planned that the award banquet be a yearly event.

The medal itself—we'd seen a photograph of it on the invitation that Lucy had received—had a bold design: a naked man and woman holding hands while riding a huge Galápagos tortoise.

And the individual the consortium had selected to receive the first medal was none other than Jack Wesley Carbondale, America's most famous living bird artist and the author of the renowned *Carbondale's Field Guides to the Birds*.

Even Lucy, who received the tickets in the mail, out of the blue, did not know why she was being invited.

The best explanation she could think of was simply that Carbondale remembered her from the Archives.

Lucy Wayles, before she became a gentlewoman birder, was director and head librarian of the world-famous Archives of Urban Natural History, now part of the Museum of Natural History.

During her tenure there, Carbondale and his assistants used the Archives when preparing new editions of their famous field guides.

Anyway, the invitation could not be refused.

As Peter Marin, himself a rather successful commercial artist, put it: "Is there really any bird-watcher alive who doesn't love the drawings of Carbondale? I doubt it. Academics love him. Avant-garde sculptors love him. Old-lady watercolorists love him. Tattoo artists love him. Even dead cubists love him."

"Stop carrying on," John Wu had cautioned. It was true: Peter always tended to extremes.

I turned east on Fifty-fifth Street and entered the park. The weather had softened. It was now an Indian summer evening.

I saw them before they saw me. All my comrades, standing together in the early evening light. Probably they were expecting me to approach via Fifty-fourth Street.

I took in the whole scene, genuinely moved. The bustling crowds. My friends and colleagues waiting for me in the park. The old-fashioned street lamps raining soft light down on the passersby. The stately hotel across the way, doormen all in braid and snap-brimmed caps.

Even the classic New York frankfurter cart at the curb with its fine yellow umbrella had taken on a romantic glow.

Peter Marin was wearing an extremely strange looking gold corduroy suit that was too small for him. However, it was a distinct improvement over his ubiquitous overalls. I am about as tolerant of the eccentricities of others as a man my age can be, but it has always puzzled me why Peter Marin chose to walk around looking like Li'l Abner.

John Wu was dressed in his usual cool, anonymously elegant gray. He was one of those people born to wear clothes and wear them well. I had trouble imagining him unclad, even as a newborn.

Willa Wayne might have just emerged from Monsieur Givenchy's salon. Her gown was classic fire-engine red, with a daring, low-plunging back that stopped a thumbnail short of . . . well, one could almost see . . . well, I hadn't seen a dress like that in many a year . . . not since that film in the 1970s, *Shampoo*, where the sight of Julie Christie's backless dress had triggered an asthmatic condition I had not even known I had before that instant.

And as for my Lucy? Oh, that was another story altogether! She took my breath away.

Lucy had allowed her usually short-cropped white hair to grow out. It is now long enough, in fact, for her to braid. And that night it was piled high on her head, in the style of Kitty the saloon girl in those old Western movies.

She wore a long black dress with a high waist, and over it, draped around her shoulders, was one of her short denim jackets—this one, rose-colored. She wore tiny black pearl earrings.

And madam's slippers . . . I looked down to see that she was wearing her ugly old rubberized birder boots.

Well, Lucy always made a statement.

My heart was bumping with joy. Lord, she was beautiful. Boots and all.

I called hello to the assembled and they turned as one.

"It's about time, Markus Bloch," Lucy said when she saw me.

At first I didn't catch the little smile playing at the corners of her mouth. I was too busy gazing at the little pink spots she had rouged on her cheeks.

"But I'm not late, Lucy," I replied defensively.

She was staring at me. In fact, they all were. I felt a bit self-conscious.

Finally, her face broke into a wonderful smile and she said, "I declare, Markus Bloch! We are quite the dandy this evening!"

I wanted to purr.

But then John Wu said, "Don't take what I'm about to say the wrong way, Markus. But that thing around your neck must be the ugliest tie I have ever seen in my life."

Willa, obviously stricken, tried to soothe my hurt feelings: "But the fabric is interesting, Markus. Highly . . . unusual silk."

"It most certainly is," Lucy interjected, and then, without skipping a beat, continued with, "Let's bite the apple," meaning, I supposed, that we should get down to business.

I detected in her "bite" a hint of Southern accent. Not the deep, broad Tennessee/Virginia eruption that came when she was angry.

No, this was just a smattering of it—to get our attention.

From where we stood, we could see the award-dinner guests entering the hotel on the Fifty-fourth Street side. Cabs and limos pulled up. There were even a few photographers snapping photos, because a deputy mayor and a famous Broadway personality were masters of ceremonies.

Lucy said, "I think we must commit to at least three. In other words, we can't even think of leaving before three speakers have gotten up and sat down again. Agreed?"

We all agreed.

Lucy continued. "Now there'll be hors d'oeuvres and drinks when we walk in. But the dinner won't be served until after all the speakers are finished and the award has been presented. Can we wait that long? Will the boredom crush us? Here's what I propose. After the third speaker, anyone who thinks an exit is warranted taps his glass twice with a fork. When three of us have tapped in confirmation, we all leave. And Markus will take us to a lovely restaurant in his neighborhood. Agreed?"

"How many taps of the fork?" Peter asked.

"Two."

"Got it. Two taps. Three agreements. Does it have to be a glass?"

"As you wish, Peter," Lucy said kindly. "Tap on anything you find."

"Are you sure we will be seated at the same table?" asked Willa.

"Of course," Lucy said. "They wouldn't dare split up Olmsted's Irregulars."

Lucy often made strange statements. Strangely optimistic ones. I was sure there couldn't have been more than two out of the five hundred guests and officials of the awards dinner who had ever even heard of Olmsted's Irregulars.

Five abreast, we started across the traffic-choked street toward the hotel entrance.

Suddenly a shadow crossed my eyes.

It was very quick. A flash. Something dark.

Then I heard a savage thud.

Willa screamed.

The sidewalk shuddered beneath our feet.

And a fountain seemed to emerge out of nowhere . . . a bubbling red geyser.

Cars screeched to a stop. People froze in their tracks.

And then the screaming really began. The whole block was echoing with cries and shrieks.

Someone had leaped from a high window at the Hilton.

He had landed on the umbrella of the frankfurter stand.

Impaled!

I felt someone pulling my arm. It was Lucy.

She quickly rounded up all the stunned Irregulars and marched us into the hotel.

Once inside, she counted heads as if we were children on a grade school outing.

I adjusted my tie. That's right. After the horror I had just seen, I could think of nothing else to do.

Lucy walked over to me and caressed my face.

"Are you all right, Markus?"

"I am a physician," I heard myself say, my voice like something from beyond the grave. "Certainly I'm all right. I was trained to deal with trauma."

"You don't look it," she said.

"It happened right in front of me!" I exploded. "Splat!"

She trapped my gesticulating hands and stilled them. "Oh, Markus, Markus."

"What?" I said.

"Beware the butcher-bird, Markus," she said softly.

"What the hell does that mean?"

She smiled her cryptic smile and headed into the party area, gently pulling me after her.

John Wu, cool and composed as you please, whispered from behind me, into my ear, "The butcher-bird is a common name for the northern shrike. It impales its victims on thorns."

Thank you, John! For nothing, as usual.

About five minutes later, as the delicious miniature pizzas I am so fond of were being served by tall, gaunt waiters, we learned that the flying object had been Jack Wesley Carbondale.

SUPER SLEUTHS

☐ **TENSLEEP** *An Em Hansen Mystery* **by Sarah Andrews.** Stuck on an oil-drilling rig in the Wyoming Badlands with a bunch of roughnecks is a tough place for a woman. But feisty, sharp-edged Emily "Em" Hansen, working as a mudlogger, calls this patch of Tensleep Sanstone home. She is about to call it deadly. "Lively ... don't miss it!"—Tony Hillerman　　　　　　　　　　　　(186060—$4.99)

☐ **HEIR CONDITION** *A Schuyler Ridgway Mystery* **by Tierney McClellan.** Schuyler Ridgway works as a real estate agent and watches videos at home alone on Saturday nights. She is definitely not having an illicit affair with the rich, elderly Ephraim Benjamin Cross and she certainly hasn't murdered him. So why has he left her a small fortune in his will? Now the Cross clan believes she's his mistress, and the police think she's his killer.　　　　　　　　　　　　　　　　　　(181441—$5.50)

☐ **FOLLOWING JANE** *A Barrett Lake Mystery* **by Shelly Singer.** Teenager Jane Wahlman had witnessed the brutal stabbing of a high school teacher in a local supermarket and then suddenly vanished. Berkeley teacher Barrett Lake will follow Jane's trail in return for a break into the private eye business—the toughest task she's ever faced.　　　　　　　　　　　　　　　　　　　　　　　　(175239—$4.50)

☐ **FINAL ATONEMENT** *A Doug Orlando Mystery* **by Steve Johnson.** Detective Doug Orlando must catch the murderer of Rabbi Avraham Rabowitz, in a case that moves from the depths of the ghetto to the highrise office of a glamor-boy real estate tycoon.
　　　　　　　　　　　　　　　　　　　　　　　　　　　　(403320—$3.99)

☐ **MURDER CAN KILL YOUR SOCIAL LIFE** *A Desiree Shapiro Mystery* **by Selma Eichler.** New York P.I., Desiree Shapiro is a chubby gumshoe who has a mind as sharp as a Cuisinart and a queen-size talent for sleuthing. She takes on the case of the poor grocery boy accused of killing the old lady in apartment 15D for the money stashed in her freezer. Before anyone can say Haagen-Dazs, Desiree bets she will be able to finger the real killer.　　　　　　　　　　　　　　　　　(181395—$5.50)

Prices slightly higher in Canada

Buy them at your local bookstore or use this convenient coupon for ordering.

PENGUIN USA
P.O. Box 999 — Dept. #17109
Bergenfield, New Jersey 07621

Please send me the books I have checked above.
I am enclosing $_____ (please add $2.00 to cover postage and handling). Send check or money order (no cash or C.O.D.'s) or charge by Mastercard or VISA (with a $15.00 minimum). Prices and numbers are subject to change without notice.

Card #_____ Exp. Date _____
Signature_____
Name_____
Address_____
City _____ State _____ Zip Code _____

For faster service when ordering by credit card call **1-800-253-6476**

Allow a minimum of 4-6 weeks for delivery. This offer is subject to change without notice.

INTRIGUING MYSTERIES BY
LYDIA ADAMSON